Anna Maria Moon

The Rev. W. Leeves, Author of the Air of Auld Robin Gray

With a Few Notices of Other Members of his Family. Second Edition

Anna Maria Moon

The Rev. W. Leeves, Author of the Air of Auld Robin Gray
With a Few Notices of Other Members of his Family. Second Edition

ISBN/EAN: 9783337277192

Printed in Europe, USA, Canada, Australia, Japan

Cover: Foto ©Raphael Reischuk / pixelio.de

More available books at **www.hansebooks.com**

In Memoriam.

THE REV. W. LEEVES,

AUTHOR OF

THE AIR OF

"AULD ROBIN GRAY."

WITH A FEW NOTICES OF OTHER MEMBERS
OF HIS FAMILY.

BY HIS GRAND-DAUGHTER A. M. MOON

(NEÉ ELSDALE).

Second Edition.

PRINTED FOR PRIVATE CIRCULATION.

JUNE 20TH, 1887.

BRIGHTON :
TUCKNOTT'S STEAM PRINTING WORKS,
KENSINGTON GARDENS.

TO A BELOVED MOTHER,

The Following Pages are

Most Affectionately Inscribed by

THE AUTHOR.

INDEX.

PREFACE.

The following pages, printed at the request of Friends, contain Reminiscences of the Rev. W. Leeves, and other Members of his Family.

Several portions of the Memoirs have formerly appeared in public print.

A revised edition of " Stray Thoughts in Verse," previously printed, is appended to the Memoirs.

The former copies of this Work bear the title, " A Family Memorial."

A. M. MOON.

104, Queen's Road, Brighton,
    June 20th, 1887.

B

A FEW

LITERARY REMAINS

AND

NOTICES OF THE LIFE

OF THE

REV. WILLIAM LEEVES.

B 2

REV. W. LEEVES AND HIS FAMILY.

William Leeves, son of Henry Leeves, Esq., of Kensington, was born June 11th, 1748. He entered His Majesty's 1st Regiment of Foot Guards, as Ensign, June 20th, 1769, and received a Lieutenant's Commission Feb. 3rd, 1772. In 1779 he took Holy Orders, and was appointed to the living of Wrington in Somersetshire, where he resided as Rector for nearly fifty years. It is a remarkable circumstance that his predecessor, the Rev. Dr. Waterland, occupied the same position for a similar period; so that the parishioners of Wrington had only two Pastors during the course of a century! The love and reverence shown to the author's Grandfather and his Family by his parishioners, which so much impressed her mind in childhood, still vividly recur to her recollection.

The memory of Dr. Waterland has ever been precious to the surviving members of his family; and judging from the esteem and veneration in which he is still held by his great grandchildren, he also must have been one of "the excellent of the earth."

The Rev. W. Leeves married Anne Wathen (third daughter of Dr. Wathen*), May 4th, 1786. She possessed great musical talent, and remarkable skill in playing the violin. They resided

---

* Dr. Wathen was a London Physician of eminence. He had three daughters. The eldest was married to Henry Wise, Esq.; the second, Katherine, to John Eckersall, Esq.; and the third, Anne, to the Rev. William Leeves.

together at Wrington for 48 years, and devoted themselves to promote, among their parishioners, harmony, love, peace, and comfort, similar to those enjoyed in their own happy and delightful home.

They had five children: William Henry, Henry Daniel, Marianne, Elizabeth, and George.

William Henry, the eldest, spent his life at Wrington, where he was born. He was "a good man, and a just." Music and Nature were his delight. He had a bass voice of surpassing power and depth, which, in leading the singing, filled the beautiful Wrington Church as with the deep rich mellow tones of an organ.

William Henry never married; and although educated for the Law, did not practice. He died at Wrington, in 1840, at the age of 53; and was interred near to the Chancel door. His tomb† is situated within a short distance of that of Mrs. Hannah More.

Henry Daniel took Holy Orders.

. Marianne was maried in 1810 to the Rev. Robinson Elsdale, D.D. (a college friend of her brother Henry, at Oxford); and annually, with her husband, visited her parents at Wrington, till their death.

Elizabeth (or "Bessy") never married, but lived with her parents to the last, soothing them in their declining years. After her mother's death in 1826, she and her brother William remained with their father, who, though afflicted by the loss of his "dear partner," was full of praise and thankfulness for his children, and the happy life and innumerable blessings he had enjoyed.

George, the youngest, with a love for the sea, became a Midshipman in the Royal Navy; but afterwards retired from the

---

† Miss E. Leeves, who died suddenly at Wrington, whilst on a visit from a distant part of the country (Brighton) in 1866, was interred in the same grave. The tomb for her brother and herself she had many years previously designed, leaving room upon it for her own inscription. Her desire to lie in the same grave with her brother was thus, in God's dispensation, signally realized.

service. He went to America, and settled there. He married an American lady, to whom he was deeply attached, and had a large family; all of whom are married. Many years after the death of his first wife, he married another American lady, who was a comfort to him in his declining days. This branch is now the only one to perpetuate the (unusual) name of Leeves, which was formerly spelt Leaves, as it appears in some parts of *Doomsday Book*, wherein the family name has been traced so far back as to the time of Edward the Confessor.

The Rev. Henry Daniel Leeves devoted a great part of his life to the spiritual and temporal welfare of the Greeks. He translated the Scriptures into the modern Greek, and distributed them (for the Bible Society) throughout the land.* At the time of the Greek Insurrection, he succoured many fugitive Greeks, concealed them in his house, saved them from death by the hands of the Turks, provided them with food and clothing, and sent them "on their way rejoicing," full of gratitude and praise. He was beloved and respected by all who knew him, and died at Beirut, whilst on his way to Jerusalem. His death was indeed the "death of the righteous."

Some time after his death, which took place in 1845, his faithful Greek Steward, Diamanti, when lying asleep in the early morning in his balcony, was shot by some Greeks.

But, alas! a deeper tragedy ensued on the night of August 28th, 1854; Mr. Leeves's son and his wife were murdered in their house at Kastaniotissa, Eubœa, by the son of the priest of the village (and others), to whom the family had shown much kindness.

On the 8th of October, their desolate and widowed mother, Mrs. Leeves, was obliged to give evidence at the trial of the murderers at Chalcis. They were condemned and executed; and all the Greeks, who were much attached to the Leeves family (particularly in memory of the Rev. H. D. Leeves), were anxious for this expiation of their crime.

---

* *Vide* p. 91.

The infant child, who was in the room at the time of the murder, was providentially preserved; but died shortly afterwards, on the 24th of November.

"AULD ROBIN GRAY."

About the year 1770, the Rev. W. Leeves, then a young Officer in the Foot Guards, of about 22 years of age, received from the Hon. Mrs. Byron, who had them from Lady Anne Lindsay, the words of " Auld Robin Gray ; " and " composed for them his beautiful Recitative and Air." These, with six Sacred Airs he dedicated in 1812, to Thomas Hammersley, Esq ; * on whose death he wrote the following lines :

> " Much-valued friend, Farewell ! The just command
> Of Him, whose cause thou hast maintain'd on earth,
> Has called thee to enjoy His blest abode !—
> To quit a family, whose tender care,
> And sweet attentions, had entwined so close
> Around a heart of sympathetic mould,
> As faintly to pourtray celestial joys.
> Yet firm thine exit !—blest with all the calmness
> A patient hope of everlasting life
> Secures to the believer. Friend, Farewell !—
> The dulcet melodies of early years
> Swell with such sweet remembrance o'er my mind,
> That I can only nurse the fond desire
> Of joining thee in *endless* harmony ! "

At Wrington, surrounded by beautiful scenery, where Locke was born, and Hannah More lived, the Author of " *Auld Robin Gray* " pursued his " happy life ;" in ministrations to his people, in literature, music, and intercourse with numerous friends. He

---

* *Vide* p. 24.

came to the close of his life, like "a shock of corn fully ripe," and was gently gathered into the heavenly garner.

May the peace which gilded his path in life, rest on ours also ; and may the remembrance of his spirit of love, in so far as he followed Christ, influence our daily walk and conversation !

The Leeves family were ever energetic in works of charity, and in the promotion of true religion ; "feeding the hungry," and "binding up the broken-hearted." Indeed, it may be said that, to them, the promises were fulfilled, "Blessed is he that considereth the poor and needy. The Lord shall deliver him in the time of trouble; the Lord will make all his bed in his sickness." So it happened to all of these. *He* was with them ; His "rod and His staff" *did* comfort them ; and with smiles of peace and joy, they passed to the mansions prepared for them in their "Father's house" above!

A. M. M.

INSCRIPTION ON A TABLET

Placed in the Chancel of Wrington Church by the REV. WILLIAM
LEEVES.

IN THIS CHANCEL ARE INTERRED THE MORTAL REMAINS OF
ANNE,
THE AMIABLE AND BELOVED WIFE OF
THE REV. WM. LEEVES, RECTOR OF THIS PARISH,
WHO DIED FEBRUARY 14TH, 1826, IN HER 71ST YEAR.
TO RECORD A
LIFE
OF HUMBLE RELIANCE ON A REDEEMER, AND A
DEATH
OF PATIENT RESIGNATION TO THE WILL OF GOD,
THIS TABLET IS ERECTED, BY HER GRATEFUL PARTNER
DURING A COURSE OF FORTY YEARS.

Of such domestic worth, in accents weak
Though strong th' impression, it were vain to speak :
This truth all must allow, with one accord,
A tender, prudent wife is from the Lord.

INSCRIPTION ON A TABLET

Formerly in the Chancel, now in the Porch of Wrington Church.

IN MEMORY OF THE
REVEREND WILLIAM LEEVES,
SON OF HENRY LEEVES, ESQ.,
WHO WAS FOR NEARLY FIFTY YEARS RECTOR OF THIS
PARISH.
His sincere piety, and the mild and conscientious tenor of his life,
secured him the respect of his parishioners, and their regret at his loss ;
whilst his surviving family remember him as the good
Father, Husband, and Master.
Music was his delight, and one of his early compositions
was the well-known air of " Auld Robin Gray."
Surrounded by his children, he died in peace and thankfulness, humbly
confiding in the merits of his Redeemer,
on the morning of Whit-Sunday, May 25, 1828, in the 80th year of his age.

IN THE SAME VAULT IN THIS CHURCH ARE INTERRED
THE REMAINS OF
ANNE LEEVES, HIS BELOVED WIFE,
DAUGHTER OF SAMUEL WATHEN, M.D.
Ardent in her feelings, benevolent and disinterested, she was the object of
warm attachment to those around her. Long and severe sufferings
tried her faith, patience, and resignation, before she was
called to her rest, on the 14th of February, 1826,
in the 71st year of her age.

ON THE DEATH OF THE REV. W. LEEVES.

"TO THE EDITOR OF THE 'BRISTOL MIRROR.'

" Sir,

"I was sorry to see the death of the Rev. Wm. Leeves *merely* mentioned in the obituary of your last paper. Such an event surely deserves some fuller memorial, and it would be naturally looked for in this city, in which he was so well known ; therefore (unless some abler pen should forestall my intention), I beg to offer a few remarks on the loss we have sustained by the departure of this amiable and highly-respected man. Mr. Leeves was Rector of Wrington (a village celebrated by having been the birthplace of Locke) for a period of nearly fifty years, and there fulfilled his clerical duties in so exemplary a manner, as to insure him the love and respect of the whole neighbour-hood. He promoted the religious and moral welfare of his flock, and was himself an example of all that is upright and good in the different relations of pastor, master, husband, and father. In performing the holy part allotted to him, there was no *display* of religion ; he followed and inculcated the sacred commandments in the true spirit of Christian meekness and humility. Mr. Leeves was never seen to greater advantage than when engaged in family worship, in which his soul delighted ; and when he became too weak to perform that duty himself, his family assembled, morning and evening, around his bed, when, in broken accents he gave the blessing. His continual and favourite amusement to the last was composing hymns, and 'singing them in his heart ;' his end was calm, tranquil, and peaceful (like the tenor of his life), and death came on almost

imperceptibly. Mr. Leeves' only earthly wish, when he felt his
end approaching, was, that he might live to see all his family
before he quitted them ; that wish was granted to him, and his
last words were, 'Resignation to the will of God.' He was
buried in the Church at Wrington ; and the inhabitants of the
village, and many of the neighbourhood, both rich and poor,
testified their respect by following his remains to the place of
interment, where a hymn was sung, to which he had been particularly partial. In the musical world, Mr. Leeves has
immortalized himself, by the exquisite and touching simplicity
of the music of the pathetic ballad of 'Auld Robin Gray,'
originally composed by him about the year 1770. This melody
has been claimed by a whole nation ; but who that was acquainted
with Mr. Leeves would question *his* word, or for a moment
believe that he would claim aught that did not belong to him ?
Perhaps one of the most convincing and sure proofs of its
authenticity lay in the modesty with which he claimed this
beautiful production, and in the characteristic simplicity with
which he acknowledged *that*, of which many would have made a
boast. When Mr. Leeves heard Miss Stephens sing this ballad,
he was so much delighted with her expression, and her melting
tones, that he shed tears. The songstress was much gratified on
hearing of the effect her singing had produced on the venerable
author, and was indulged in her wish of being introduced to the
composer of the air which added so much to her celebrity.
But there are so many anecdotes connected with this subject,
doubtless well known, that I need not repeat them. Mr. Leeves
composed much sacred music, some of which is already in print,
and it is to be hoped that what he has left may be laid before
the public. At a very advanced age his voice, though feeble,
was harmonious, and could not be heard without exciting
feelings of deep emotion. Mr. Leeves also possessed the gift of
numbers, and his poetical productions, whether playful or
serious, always combined both taste and feeling.

" I remain, Sir, with respect, yours,

"June 5th, 1828." "E. G.

"AULD ROBIN GRAY."

" The verses for the old air were written in 1770 or 1772, by Lady Anne Lindsay, eldest daughter of the Earl of Balcarras. A highly popular air to the same words was composed by the Rev. W. Leeves, Rector of Wrington, Somersetshire. He tells us that, in 1770, having received a copy of the verses from the Hon. Mrs. Byron, he immediately set them to music; but in a letter from Lady Anne Lindsay (then Barnard) to Sir Walter Scott in July, 1823, she says she composed the song ' soon after the close of the year 1771 !' She or Mr. Leeves may have mistaken the year. Although not a Scottish melody, Mr. Leeves' air is given here on account of its great popularity."

[Taken from "The Songs of Scotland," adapted to their appropriate melodies. Illustrated with historical, biographical, and critical notices. By George Farquhar Graham.]

"AULD ROBIN GRAY."

Extract from a Newspaper, October, 1843.

" Miss Adelaide Kemble sang this ballad at her benefit on Tuesday night at Covent Garden. Miss Birch sang it at Mr. Fletcher's concert on Thursday; and Mr. Wilson had the honour of singing it before the Queen in Scotland, and has since given it everywhere else in his tour through the provinces. Now, many of these persons who sang this ballad, and many more who listened to it, have thought all the while they were singing or listening to genuine Scottish music, and an old Scottish ballad that had existed from the time they knew not when. No such thing. This air was originally and entirely composed by the Rev. William Leeves (who died only a few

years ago), rector of Wrington in Somerset, and the friend and
constant visitor of Mrs. Hannah More, at Barley Wood, in the
same parish, where the writer of this notice has often met both
parties, and some of whose most pleasing reminiscences are
associated with the old Rectory House at Wrington, and its
venerable and much loved inmates. The son of this Mr. Leeves
has long been settled at Athens, and some of our readers have,
we dare say, contributed to the church which his and their
means have conjoined to raise, and of which he is the zealous
minister. It was the father of this Mr. Leeves, the Athenian,
who, once a gay officer in the guards, but afterwards, as we
have said, the excellent and respected rector of Wrington,
having a great talent for music, on receiving the words of
'Auld Robin Gray' at the hands of Lady Anne Lindsay, at
her ladyship's special request (we believe there was a little
wager pending, relating to the possibility or not of imitating
closely Scottish music), produced the beautiful ballad which
is now the theme of universal admiration, and as universally
believed to be an original old air from the north of the
Tweed; for Mr. Leeves (giving himself up to the duties of
his parish, and recreating himself with his violoncello and the
composition of sacred music) gave no heed to the pirated
editions which were springing up on all sides, and as little
attention to the sensation it caused in the world. But in late
years, at the earnest solicitation of his friends, seconded, we
believe, by Miss Stephens, his great favourite, who knew and
venerated the composer, and from whom she received several
judicious hints as to the best manner of giving effect to this
ballad, he consented to publish it with his name, and the history
and proof of its original composition by him prefixed. In this
publication six sacred songs are added, several of which are
productions of very considerable merit and great beauty. We
know not whether the volume be out of print or not."

"LETTER AND PREFACE

" *To Six Sacred Compositions and 'Auld Robin Gray,'*
by the REV. W. LEEVES.

" To THOMAS HAMMERSLEY, ESQ.

" My dear Sir,

" Anxious as you have ever been for the rule of right, as
well as for the fair fame of your friends, you have more than
once solicited that I would publicly claim an offspring which,
for more than forty years has been of uncertain origin. Nothing
could have induced me to undertake this at my period of life, but
the offer of your kind testimony to the genuineness of this my
early production, which an acquaintance with it in manuscript,
long before it surreptitiously found its way to the public eye,
enables you so convincingly to bear. As to the story, you may
remember that I received it from the Hon. Mrs. Byron, and
understood it to have been written by Lady Anne Lindsay ; but
lest it may be supposed that lyrics have engrossed more than a
proper share of my attention, I adjoin some sacred compositions,
and submit the whole to your protection. These, I hope, may
not be an uninteresting addition, at a time when the spirit of
religion in this country is happily on the increase.

" Believe me, with much esteem,
" My dear Sir,
" Your very sincere and obliged,
" WM. LEEVES.
" Wrington, June 12, 1812."

PREFACE.

" The Amateur Author of this little Collection would be
sorry that any idea of incongruity should attach to the
association of what is entitled a *Ballad*, with compositions
avowedly *sacred*. The latter he ventures to offer *professionally*,
at a period when a taste for Religion is no longer the only one

left uncultivated. The former ought not to be esteemed inconsistent with subjects of a serious nature, when it is recollected that the term *Ballad* (according to DR. WATTS) 'once signified a solemn and sacred song'—that dignity of style and tenderness of expression are mutually the characteristics of sacred music and of the original Scottish melody; and above all, that the catastrophe of this particular Ballad is evidently marked by that most essential Christian grace, *resignation*. A high encomium is conceived to have been conferred on this imitation of the ancient strains of Minstrelsy, by the unwillingness to believe that it is a modern production. Some mistake may have arisen from the existence of a Scotch song, adapted to these words, the antiquity of which has in vain been endeavoured to be ascertained; but the enquiry has produced the following very satisfactory light upon the subject, from an ingenious and respectable Gentleman at Edinburgh.

'It is almost impossible to ascertain at what precise time, or 'by whom, any of the Scottish airs were composed. Some of 'our musical antiquaries, particularly the late MR. TITLER, 'endeavoured, by a critical examination of the structure of the 'Airs, to fix the æras of their production; but he gives fancies 'and conjectures merely, instead of anything like evidence; and 'his Dissertation, which is annexed to Arnot's History of 'Edinburgh, is altogether unsatisfactory. The origin of our 'music is extremely uncertain, though there are various circum- 'stances which nearly convince me that it cannot be so ancient 'as some of our zealous countrymen think it. With respect to 'the old Air of 'Auld Robin Gray,' I conceive it to be more 'modern than many of the Scottish Airs, because in Ramsay's 'Tea-Table Miscellany, first published about 1724, it is not 'mentioned.'

"This Air is printed as an introduction to that now published in the celebrated DR. HAYDN's Collection of National Melodies. As the *measure* is of a similar nature, it may not be unsatisfactory to declare, which can be done with the clearest conscience, that the Editor of the present publication never

C

heard of any other music than his own, being applied to
these interesting words, till many years after that was produced
to which he now asserts an undivided claim. From the
preceeding Address to his now, alas! much lamented friend,
MR. HAMMERSLEY, to whom this work was intended to have
been affectionately inscribed, it appears that *he* was well
acquainted with this Ballad long before its surreptitious appearance in print; and the still more convincing testimony might
be added, of a respectable relative now resident at Bath, who
was on a visit to the Author's family at Richmond, when the
words were received and the first manuscript produced. That
this little attempt was never intended as an imposture on the
Musical World, the open acknowledgment of it at the time it first
appeared will sufficiently prove ; and it may perhaps be esteemed
a further collateral evidence, that the only remuneration hitherto
received by the real composer of what is termed the *modern*
'Auld Robin Gray,' so often sung, and so repeatedly sold, has
been,—what he values, however, most highly,—the candid
approbation of his private Friends."

THE WELL KNOWN BALLAD

AULD ROBIN GRAY.

as originally composed about the year 1770 by the

REV^d WILLIAM LEEVES.

Words by Lady Ann Lindsay

When the sheep are in the fauld and the kye at hame,   And a' the warld to sleep is gane;

The waes o' my heart fall in showers fra my ee,   When my gude man is sound by me.

V.S.

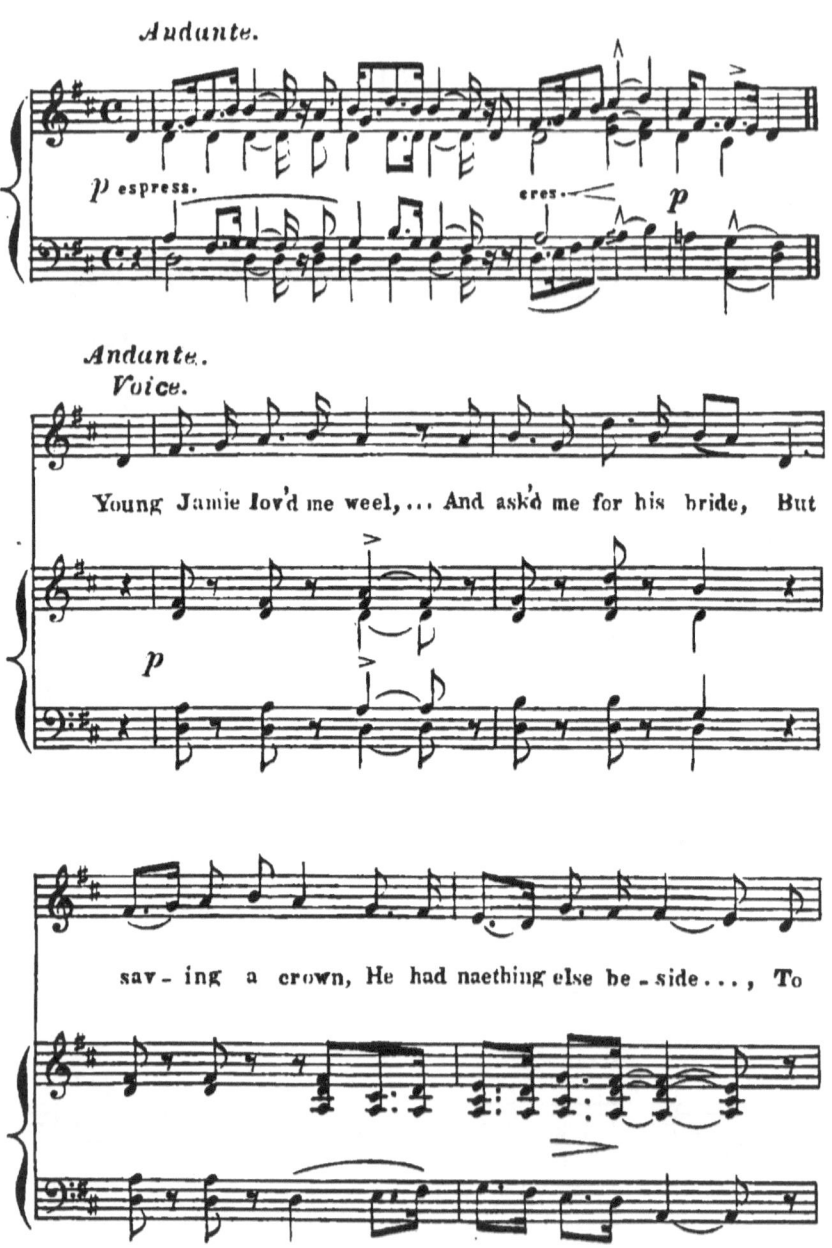

Young Jamie lov'd me weel, ... And ask'd me for his bride, But

sav - ing a crown, He had naething else be - side ..., To

make the crown a pound my Ja_mie went to sea, And the

p

p sostenuto.

crown and the pound were baith for me. He had nae been gane but a

p

year and a day, When my Faither brake his arm, and our

cres.

pp

cow was stole, a－way: My Mither she fell sick,.. and

Jamie at the sea, And Auld Ro-bin Gray came a-

court--ing to me.

AULD ROBIN GRAY.

RECITATIVE.

" When the sheep are in the fauld, and the kye at hame,
And a' the warld to sleep is gane ;
The waes o' my heart fall in showers fra my e'e,
When my gude man is sound by me.

" Young Jamie lov'd me weel, and ask'd me for his bride,
But saving a crown, he had naething else beside ;
To make the crown a pound my Jamie went to sea,
And the crown and the pound were baith for me.
He had nae been gane but a year and a day,
When my faither brake his arm, and our cow was stole away :
My mither she fell sick, and Jamie at the sea,
And Auld Robin Gray came a-courting to me.

" My faither could nae work, my mither could nae spin,
I toil'd day and night, but their bread I could nae win ;
Auld Rob maintain'd 'em baith, and wi' tears in his e'e,
Said, ' Jeany, for *their* sakes, O marry me ! '
My heart it said nae, and I look'd for Jamie back ;
But the wind it blew hard, and his ship was a wrack ;—
His ship it was a wrack,—why did nae Jeany dee ?
And why do I live to cry, ' Wae is me ? '

" My faither urg'd me sair,—my mither did nae speak,
But she look'd in my face, till my heart was like to break ;
They gi'ed him my hand, but my heart was at the sea ;
Sae Auld Robin Gray is gude man to me.

C 2

I had nae been a wife but weeks only four,
When sitting sae mournfully at my ain door,
I saw my Jamie's wraith,—for I could nae think it he,
Till he said, ' I'm come hame, love, to marry thee!'

" Sair, sair did we greet, and mickle did we say :
We took but ae kiss, and we tore oursels away.
I wish that I were dead!—but I'm nae like to dee ;
Ah! why was I born to cry, ' Wae is me ? '—
I gang like a ghaist, and I care nae to spin ;
I dare nae think o'Jamie, for that would be a sin ;—
Sae I'll do my best a gude wife to be,
For Auld Robin Gray is kind to me."

Extracts from a few of Mrs. Hannah More's Letters.

Extract from a letter to Mrs. Leeves.

"Bath, April 1, 1802.

"I thank God that I am enabled to say that I felt much peace and resignation in the near view, as all thought, of death. I believe it requires almost more Christian fortitude to bear many of the trials of life, than to meet the approaches of its dissolution. One short petition, however, should form the Christian's motto,—'Thy will be done.' Almost our whole duty seems involved in these little words. As soon as she came to Bath, I had the great pleasure of a kind visit from Mrs. Wathen. She looked delightfully. Her accounts of you did not quite equal my hope and expectation. I am thoroughly pleased at your becoming our Barley Wood neighbours, as I was half afraid of some churlish strangers. I have not yet allowed my imagination to wander to my own pretty ground, not expecting to see it again. I would not let even my thoughts attach themselves to it; I now begin to think how pretty it is. I am much obliged by Mr. Leeves' occasional inspection. How wicked to have run on so long without adverting to the blessed event of *peace ratified!* The only way in which *I* can express my satisfaction, is to treat with a good dinner both your poor-houses. . . . My sisters join me in kind regards to Mr. L. and yourself. I hope the dear little maid is better. With cordial wishes for your recovery,

"Believe me, my dear Mrs. Leeves, ·

"Very sincerely yours,

"H. MORE."

To MRS. LEEVES, *on her Mother's* (MRS. WATHEN'S) *death.*

"Thursday, April 8, 1807.
"My dear Madam,
"I do not condole with you, for it would not be just. I do not congratulate you, for it would not be decent; but I truly sympathize with you in the affecting event. Death, under such circumstances, seems divested of his terrors. She is at peace ; gone to the resting-place of the just. May we all be reminded by her death to prepare for our own. With kind regards to Mr. Leeves,

"Believe me, dear Madam,
"Very faithfully yours,
"Barley Wood."   "H. MORE.

To MISS LEEVES *(afterwards* MRS. ELSDALE*) before her Marriage.*

"My dear Miss Leeves,
"Accept from an old friend these little memorials of affection. It is some pleasure to me to hope that you and yours may be perusing them when the author is mouldered in the dust. Accept my most cordial wishes for your happiness, and that of him to whom you must owe so large a part of it. May it please God to enable you to fulfil all your religious and domestic duties in the most exemplary manner. That *He* may direct, bless, and sanctify you by His grace, is the sincere wish of your very affectionate friend,

"HANNAH MORE.
"Barley Wood, 21st July, 1810."

To the REV. WM. LEEVES, *after her last Sister's death.*

"To the Rev. Wm. Leeves,
"I am exceedingly obliged and gratified by the affecting attentions, both of Father and Son, in the public services of the

day. With a trembling hand, and ever-oppressed heart, I could not forbear sending these poor thanks, and desiring your prayers for your obliged and affectionate,

"H. MORE.

" Return the enclosed by the bearer.*

" Sunday Evening, Sept. 1819."

* A letter just arrived from the Bishop of Gloucester requesting that himself and Mr. Wilberforce might attend the funeral.

EXTRACT FROM A SERMON

Preached by the REV. HENRY D. LEEVES, *at Wrington Church, after the Death of his Father, the* REV. W. LEEVES, *who died on Whitsunday, May* 20*th,* 1828, *at the age of* 80.

1 COR. ix. 24, 25.

＊　　　＊　　　＊

" These are the last words to you my brethren, of your aged Minister, before he gave up his soul to God. I *will hope* that you will bear them away with you in your hearts, and that they will excite many of you—(nay, I will utter a large hope, for my heart is open towards you)—that they will excite *all of you* to consider your ways, and henceforth so to run, that you may obtain an incorruptible crown, and ' shine as the sun in the kingdom of your heavenly Father.'

" As to him who wrote these words, I humbly trust that, through the merits of our Redeemer, he is gone to partake of that inheritance of pure joy which it was his earnest desire to excite you to seek. After a long, and as he used gratefully to acknowledge, a peculiarly tranquil and happy life (nearly fifty years of which were spent among you in this parish), he has passed through as peculiarly a tranquil and happy death, into the presence of his Lord.

" It would ill become me, standing in the near relation in which I do to our dear departed father and friend, to enter into any laboured panegyric of his character and conduct. During a long period of years, his life has been before you ; and in the situation which he filled as a Minister of Christ, he has been as ' a city on a hill, which cannot be hid.' It should, therefore, be rather for *you* to *testify*, than for *me* to *assert*, that he has shown forth amongst you the fruits of a real Christianity, in a pious, humble, charitable, forbearing, meek, upright and consistent course of conduct. I believe, indeed, there will be few among you, whose hearts will not be saying at this moment,—' He was a good man, and he is gone to his rest ; may God give me grace to follow him.' And if such be the thought of your hearts, I would join to it my hearty Amen. May God give us all grace to follow him !

" But though his life has thus been before you, and calls not on me to speak of it, it may not be uninteresting to you to hear,—and indeed, as his flock, you have a sort of right to learn,—some particulars concerning the last days of his existence, after he was withdrawn from your observation. Very soon after his last appearance in this pulpit, to which exertion he was evidently unequal, another attack of his complaint seized him, from which it was apparent, both to those around him and to himself, that in his weakened state he could not recover. He then desired that his absent children might be sent for, whom he expressed an anxiety to see once more ; ' and after that,' he said, ' I hope I shall be allowed to say,— Lord, now lettest Thou Thy servant depart in peace.'

" It pleased God to hear and fulfil this his wish, I think, in its fullest extent ; and to grant at the same time to his Family the consolation of seeing their Parent pass out of this world without pain of body, and in tranquility of mind, through the exercise of a truly Christian faith, and hope, and resignation to the will of God. It pleased God, indeed, to remove from him all fear whatever of death. He met it, and made all his preparations for it with the calmness with which a man would order his affairs for a long journey; and as death approached nearer and nearer, he hailed its coming as a friend,—frequently expressed his desire to depart,—and rejoiced at perceiving his increasing weakness, as bringing him nearer to the haven of rest, where he would be. Yet he showed no impatience. 'I trust,' he said, 'I can wait God's time with perfect resignation.' Nor could anything be further from him than a presumptuous confidence, or a reliance on his own merits; for, indeed, *humility* was a feature which strongly marked his character. 'I am fully conscious,' he would say, 'of my *numberless transgressions;* but I have a *good hope* that they are *all blotted out*, through the merits and propitiation of my blessed Saviour Jesus Christ. In *Him alone* can we trust.' And often did he repeat the same words,—'In *Him alone* can we trust.'

"He frequently expressed his thankfulness to Almighty God for the many blessings he had been permitted to enjoy in this world, saying that 'his life had been a life of mercies from its very beginning to its end;' and he was particularly grateful for the *nature* of his illness, and the easy manner in which he was permitted, as he expressed it, to 'slide out of this world,' in considering which, he would often exclaim that it was 'wonderful,' that it was 'a merciful dispensation.'

"The thought of the dear partner of his life, who had gone before him, always filled him with tender and animated recollections, and the hope of being re-united with her formed a part of his prospects of enjoyment in a better world. 'I trust,' he said, 'I am going to rejoin my dear partner in peace and happiness;' and in almost his last moments, when speaking of her, he said, 'I *trust* we shall meet to *part* no more.'

"Among the books in which, during the last months of his life, he took the greatest pleasure, and which he would frequently recommend, was one entitled, 'On the four last things —Death and Judgment, Heaven and Hell;' and his mark was found standing at a prayer it contains 'for a holy and happy death,'—a prayer which he both used in private and in his family devotions, which he performed himself as long as his strength permitted him. When he became unequal to this task, he regularly called his family to prayers around his bed, in which he fervently joined, and scarcely ever failed to close them himself, though in weak and broken accents, with that beautiful benediction in the office for the Visitation of the Sick,—which comprises also the last text on which he addressed you from this pulpit,—'The Lord be merciful to us and bless us, and cause His face to shine upon us, and be gracious unto us; the Lord lift up the light of His countenance upon us, and give us *peace now and evermore:*' and the words '*Peace now and evermore*' were often on his lips, particularly during the closing hours of his life. Among the last words he was able distinctly to utter, was the Apostolic benediction,—which was indeed a solemn and consoling farewell to us all,—' The grace of our Lord Jesus Christ, and the love of God, and the fellowship of the Holy Ghost, be with us all;' repeating again, with strong emphasis, 'be with *us all evermore.*' Then shortly after, he settled himself into a tranquil and composed attitude, and with his head leaning on his hand, and a countenance indicating no pain or uneasiness, gently and gradually breathed out his spirit into the hands of his ' faithful Creator, and most merciful Saviour.'

"And now, my brethren, may we not say, in the words of the Thanksgiving in our Liturgy, 'We bless, O Lord, Thy holy name for this Thy servant who has departed this life in Thy faith and fear; beseeching Thee to give us grace so to follow his good example, that with him we may be partakers of Thy heavenly kingdom. Grant this, O Lord, for Jesus Christ's sake. Amen.' "

THE LAST DAYS

Of the REV. W. LEEVES, *given in a few particulars by his eldest*
DAUGHTER (MRS. ELSDALE).

" May, 1828.

"Tuesday evening, May 13, I reached the rectory. A
deeply interesting meeting: in the first place, with a dear brother
(Henry), after nine years separation ; my father extremely weak,
and only just able to speak to me, but with his usual affection.
I asked him if he suffered pain. He said 'No; I am mercifully
dealt with, mercifully dealt with ;' and stated the chief suffering
of body which oppressed him. He slept much during the night.

"Wednesday morning, 14th. The children were brought
into his room, and he blessed them individually, laying his hand
upon their heads, and exhorting them to be good. He was so
exhausted with this, that he felt it necessary to delay a little the
receiving of the Lord's Supper. At four o'clock we all
assembled,—his five children and four servants,—to partake with
him. It was a highly interesting scene. My aged father commenced by imploring God to render what we were about to hear
and to receive profitable to all present; and at the conclusion,
uttered these beautiful words: 'God be merciful to us and bless
us, and send the light of His countenance upon us, and give us
peace, both now and evermore ;' to which we added our hearty
'Amen.' He spoke kindly to the servants, and bid them
farewell. Then he called each of his children by name, kissed
and blessed us, and spoke much of 'the comfort the scene had
afforded him ; the satisfaction of seeing us around him ; and
receiving the Holy Supper from a dear son. He was now ready
to depart: the sooner he was released, if it pleased God, the
better.' His freedom from anything like dread of death was
astonishing.

"Friday morning, 16th. We had prayers in my father's room. He entered into them fully, giving his hearty 'Amen and Amen.' He was taken out of bed, was apparently rather better, and talked a good deal. He slept from three till nine (usually he was very restless), when he took some tea, and then he wished for prayers again, saying, after the fatigue of moving him, 'Now let me be quiet for five minutes, and then I shall be able, I hope, to unite fervently.' When I had been doing something for him, he kissed me, and said, 'God bless you, and thank you.' When Henry had been moving him, he said, 'Remember Anchises.' Henry said, 'These bodily uneasinesses will only serve to render the rest of heaven more delightful.' 'Oh, yes,' he replied, 'the nearer I approach to my last hour, the delight seems not to be conceived.' His constant restlessness, at length, this night, terminated in sleep. Henry and I sat up with him till three. He said, 'Henry, can't you read me a few sentences?'—and he read some psalms until he was composed, happily, to sleep.

"Saturday, 17th. About one o'clock, we all assembled to prayers in his room ; he had asked for them twice before, but all of us were not ready, and he dropped to sleep. . I asked him how he felt. He said, 'I have had a good deal to struggle with this morning,—against weakness, against distaste for all nourishment, and other trying feelings ; but if I can but get to the right place at last, all this will not signify.' Then he added, 'I am quite ready, my dears, to unite with you ;' and during Henry's prayers, he often shewed the spirit and truth with which he entered into them. He always, though inarticulately, repeated the Lord's Prayer ; and then he closed all in an affecting manner, by deliberately pronouncing, 'The Lord bless us, and keep us ; the Lord make His face to shine upon us ; the Lord lift up the light of His countenance upon us, and give us peace, and in the end eternal life. Amen.' He then spoke a little to Henry on the calmness and peace he enjoyed, and on the 'comfort of having,' as he pleased to express it, '*such* a family around him. It cannot but fill me with great gratitude ;

sure never man had such comforts in this world.' Prayers again in the evening; and he said, ' May God grant that such prayers offered in such a manner, may have their effect upon my soul!' Our dear father said to-night, 'I hope I am growing weaker; but it is very gradual.'

"Sunday, 18th. He appeared weaker, both in spirit and body. I sat up with my dear father. I had been some time administering to his little wants, and he thanked me once or twice. At length, he said, ' What a plague I am to you, my dear,—an old man, that is not worth twopence; the sooner 'tis over the better.' I replied, ' We must patiently wait the Almighty's will; we count nothing a trouble for so valued a parent; but human aid is of little avail.' ' Oh no; the true comfort is in a firm reliance on my suffering Saviour. I must endeavour to bear it ; and what, indeed, are my pains, compared to those intense ones of my dear Saviour! Oh, dear, they are nothing. I only fear they are too little. And now God bless you my dear.' ' I hoped he felt disposed for sleep.' ' Yes, I hope so ; but at least to meditate in quiet.'

"Tuesday morning, 20th. We had prayers in my father's room. This was his delight. He afterwards devoutly said, ' May the Lord enable me to bear with patience all He lays upon me ; and when my time of dismissal arrives, to say, Lord, now lettest Thou Thy servant depart in peace, for mine eyes have seen Thy salvation.' When moved on to the sofa, to have his bed made, he sweetly slept, and in a dream exclaimed, ' Oh, how beautiful ! '

" May 22nd and 23rd he appeared better.

" Friday night, the 24th, about twelve, he had a harassing fit of coughing and phlegm, and was quite exhausted, but slept from two o'clock the chief part of the night, and scarcely awoke till eleven o'clock on Saturday morning, when we all came around him, seeing him especially feeble. We were just going to family prayers below, but did not feel disposed to leave him, as he seemed to be drawing near his last hour. When Henry looked at him, I think he uttered, ' mercy ; ' and though he

could but feebly speak, he united in prayer, and was perfectly
conscious of all that passed. He attempted to join in the
Lord's Prayer, and was evidently fervent in holy aspirations.
When Henry had concluded, my father uttered some words
about 'peace.' Henry said, 'I hope, my dear father, you ex-
perience this peace.' He said, 'I hope so;' then, after a little,
he with difficulty pronounced 'The grace of our Lord Jesus
Christ,' &c., and twice repeated ' be with us *all*,' with a particular
emphasis on the last word. He also requested all our prayers.
Henry said he was sure we were all praying for him in our hearts ;
to which he replied, 'I hope so.' I was left alone with him for
a short time ; he said, 'Where are all the rest ?' They all came ;
and our dear Henry, who was a great blessing to him, spoke
much to him. He said he 'saw us faintly, but he comprehended
all we said.' When asked if he gave us all his blessing: 'I do
most heartily ; and the same to my dear absent son, George.'
To the two little Henrys, standing by his bed, he held up his
hand in token that he blessed them. My little Henry went away
in a flood of tears, and locked himself in my room. Henry
prayed again with and for our dear parent, who comforted us, and
deeply touched us, by the calm sweet hope which he expressed.
His only confidence was in Jesus. He said many times, 'I trust
to be saved only through the infinite merits of Christ Jesus my
Lord.' Something he said, 'with all my heart, for Jesus' sake,'
I could not make out. In answer to a prayer, in which our dear
mother was mentioned, he murmured, when almost past utterance,
'Amen ;' and then said, 'I trust to meet her in heaven to part
no more.' Henry said, 'No pain, I hope ?' 'No ; I thank God.'
'Nor fear ?'—'I hope not.' And then again he expressed his
firm hope and trust *alone* in a gracious Saviour. About half-
past six, Henry addressed some passages of Scripture to him,
which, for the first time, he appeared not to notice. Henry said,
'I hope I do not trouble you;' he said indistinctly, 'No.'
Henry said, 'Do you hear me ?'—he made a motion that he did.
Henry then said, 'I, for my own part, feel uncommonly thankful
to God, my merciful God, for having brought me home to

behold my dear father once again ; and above all, to witness this
calm and tranquil scene.' Here our dear parent made an effort
to speak, but in vain ; and we then thought it our duty not to
say anything more to him, lest it should disturb his evidently
departing spirit. With his left hand under his cheek, he seemed
as if tranquilly going to rest in sleep. Henry (who was a sweet
ministering comforter) said, ' Going to sleep in Jesus ; and we
hope, to wake to a joyful resurrection.' We echoed our prayers,
and our dear father's eyes were lifted up to heaven in supplication.
A melting scene ! He now ceased to speak or to notice us ; his
breathing became more short, and his pulse scarcely perceptible.
His appearance reminded us of the startled, convulsive sleep of
a sick infant. He continued thus till near a quarter before three
on the morning of Whitsunday, when he breathed his last,
surrounded only by five of his children, Sophia Leeves being
included. Dear George was absent in America. Two of those
left have since been called away : William,—honest William,—
on the 15th of July, 1840, and beloved and blessed Henry Daniel,
on May 8th, 1845, who had so tenderly smoothed an earthly
father's dying pillow. May we that remain be *ready* when our
Lord shall call !

"M. E.

"London, Sept., 1846."

A FEW EXTRACTS

From the Notes of MR. LEEVES' *youngest* DAUGHTER (MISS E. LEEVES), *during his last illness.* 1828.

"May 2. When humming a bar of 'On stillness, emblem meet of death,' one of his late compositions, my father said, 'In the night watches I sing it over to myself very comfortably.'— 'With your own ideas of expression!' He smiled, and said, 'No performer ever satisfied me.' He asked before for Handel's 'Holy! Holy!'—in all his illness a solace; I sang it as well as I could, and heard him from his room exclaim, 'Delightful!' He was in a state of tranquil thankfulness, saying, 'It is hard to complain of the cook, when I have lost both taste and appetite.'

"5th. After arranging him for the night, he said, 'If it please the Almighty to call me now, I am as much prepared to meet my God now, as five years hence.' He spoke of the clerical profession, and said 'it would be a great cut-up for his family, who must leave their home.' I said 'it was a delightful profession worth taking 'for better for worse;' I had spent a very happy life here.'

"6th. William and I sang at his desire, 'What is life?' He joined in, and seemed cheered, and said, 'Very good,— delightful;' I told him he 'seemed refreshed as a flower after a shower.'

"7th. Miss Thornton saw him raising his hand and beating time in his sleep, as he dozed on the sofa.

"8th. He said, ''Thank God, I passed a very comfortable night. My great friend, just now, is sleep. Ah! do go and enjoy yourself.' I replied, 'I always enjoy myself.'

The Rev. A. Perry read part of the 'Visitation for the Sick.' After William had given the blessing, he observed to the servants, 'So live together here on earth, so as to obtain *everlasting life*,—if we can all do that!'

"12th. I asked if 'he felt any pain?' He said, 'No; wonderful, merciful dispensation!' When turning round upon his side to go to sleep, surprised at his weakness, he looked up to heaven, and said, 'I trust I am going to rejoin my dear partner in peace and happiness.' I observed, 'You look very like my mother.' 'Ah,' he replied, '*I hope I shall be like her*, and enjoy the perfection of harmony together!' I continued, 'And have your taste for music gratified.' He replied, 'Ah, mine has been a *taste* indeed!'

"15th. Mr. P. asked him if 'he suffered much pain?' He replied, ' Pain!—pain, with such an amiable family around me, vying with each other to make me comfortable!'

"25th. His pulse was feeble; I sent for Henry: we all surrounded his bed, and went to prayers with him. Though scarcely able to speak, he perfectly entered into what was going on, lifting up his eyes at different parts, and saying, 'Amen— A-men.' Afterwards, his lips moved in prayer, and he was able to articulate, 'Forgive,—Jesus Christ,—through Jesus Christ.' 'Grace of our Lord Jesus Christ—love of God—fellowship of the Holy Ghost—be with us all—be with us all!' Henry asked him if 'he felt pain?' He replied, 'Thank God, no pain;— weakness—debility;—but resi—resig—nation to the—will of —God!'

"26th. I held his hand, my fingers rested on his pulse—it beat feebly, then stopped; beat again once more—again stopped: a few more beats,—then ceased for ever!

"A FAMILY OF LOVE."
"Whitsunday."   "E. L.

D

EXTRACT FROM A SERMON

Preached at the Ambassador's Chapel at Constantinople, by the
REV. H. D. LEEVES, *after hearing of the decease of his Mother.*
1826.

PSALM xxiii. 1, 2, 3, 4.

*   *   *

"'The heart of the wise is in the house of mourning'
(Eccles. vii. 2, 3, 4). Influenced by such thoughts, and in the
hope that the contemplation of such a subject may be neither
useless nor uninteresting to you, permit me to lay before you
some details of the last hours of one, who through life was a
most affectionate and faithful wife, the tenderest of mothers,
and, without any pretension, a truly benevolent, active, and
pious Christian ; and who has left, in the closing scene of her
days, a memorial of resigned patience under suffering, of
affectionate interest for her family and all around, of love
towards her fellow-creatures, and of humble yet joyful hope in
her God and Saviour, which has drawn the sting from the
grief her family cannot but feel at her loss, and left to us all
the truest, the most delightful consolation.

"For several years past, her life had been one of much
suffering, and the bodily anguish she endured in the termination
of her fatal illness was extreme. Long familiarised to the view
of death, her great anxiety was to depart, and to behold, face
to face, that Saviour in whom she trusted ; yet she constantly
checked all impatient desires of release. On the Friday night
before her death, says one of my family, waking up to a sense
of her sorrowful state, she implored mercy of her Redeemer,
and fervently entreated to be released from her sufferings, which
she exclaimed were dreadful ; but immediately checking herself,
and looking sweetly composed, she said, ' But I bow with low
submission, with *low submission.* Thy will be done, O Lord.'

She desired one of her dearest friends to be told 'that she prayed not so much for relief from her sufferings, as for patience under them;' and on one of these occasions of anguish she said, 'But not one pain too much, for the greatness of the reward,'—and looking upward she smiled radiantly twice, with a brightened eye, as if she really caught a glimpse of the termination of those 'short afflictions, which should work out an eternal weight of glory.' 'I hope,' she said to those around her, 'I hope you will look upon me with satisfaction when I am dead,—happy, I trust, and free from pain, through the merits of my Saviour, my *beautiful* Saviour; His face, *His* face to cheer me.'

"That tender affection for her husband and children, which formed at all times a distinguishing feature of her character, shone bright and strong to the last. When washing her hands in preparation for the sacrament, she looked on her wedding-ring and said, with a bright smile, 'It has not been a chain to me!'— and 'I shall never forget,' says my afflicted father, 'the tone and look with which she said, 'Not know *him!*' when asked, at my approach, if she knew who it was; nor the playful manner in which she drew her ring from her finger, and placed it on mine, saying, 'now she would marry me, as I had done her so many years ago.' 'You will not be surprised,' he adds, 'at my resolve, that this shall go with me to the grave, which I am now erecting for us both in my own chancel.'

"Her affectionate expressions concerning her absent children, whom not to see before she quitted this world was among her greatest trials, I shall not venture to repeat. But it has been my consolation to know that, as this tender mother got a nearer view of the heavenly world, her painful longings after them appeared to subside, and she seemed satisfied that we should meet and know each other in a future state.

"To all her attendants she repeatedly expressed her gratitude for their anxious attentions to her, giving them salutary advice, and hoping that the situation they now saw her in, as a dying woman, would be of service to them!

D 2

" Her religion seemed to show itself in love to all her fellow-creatures ; and to her purified mind, the beauties of nature still retained all their charm. One of her children said to her, ' I think you seem to love all mankind, my dear mother.' ' I do,' she replied ; ' and pray tell all those who enquire about me, that I am much obliged to them, and wish them well.' She often had the sash of her window open to look into the garden. One morning she heard the children playing in the fields ; she smiled, and said, ' Some more of my fellow-creatures.' She was delighted with the singing of the birds. 'I observed to her,' said the same individual, ' that it put me in mind of one of our morning prayers, which began, ' The birds of the air salute the rising sun with their cheerful voices ; much more should we return Thee our unfeigned acknowledgments.' 'Ah !' she said, ' I like to hear about prayer ; let me hear *more* about it, let my mind be filled with such sweet subjects.' And here let me observe that prayer was indeed her great delight and resource ; that by which her sufferings were lightened, by which she soared above this earth, and obtained a foretaste of those heavenly joys, for which God was, through painful, though wise trials, preparing her.

"In ease and in health, my brethren,—in the tumult of worldly pleasures or worldly cares, poor and unsatisfying as they are,—we too much neglect this necessary duty, this high privilege of prayer ; but the time must come when we shall all fly to it as our resource : and should we not fear, lest, if we now neglect our God, He may then in our hour of need not hear us ? But I will no longer dwell on this subject, except to express my confident hope, my assured belief, that God *did* hear *her* prayers ; and that, having been purified and perfected through sufferings,—sufferings which were not testimonies of God's anger, but of His mercy ; for 'whom the Lord loveth, He chasteneth,'—she, in breathing her last sigh in this world, entered into those joys which seen by the eye of faith, had cheered her bed of sickness, and made death appear a messenger of peace.

"And now, my brethren, I entreat you to pardon me should any of you think that I have too rudely drawn aside the veil of the chamber of death, or lightly betrayed the sanctity of domestic sorrow and consolation. I seem myself to have found my excuse in the belief, that I have set before you no unamiable picture of the influence of true religion on those hours to which we must all come, and in the persuasion I feel that the death-bed of the Christian-is the best lesson to the human heart.

"It has been a custom among barbarous nations to sacrifice human victims at the funeral pile of deceased parents or honoured friends. I would desire a nobler and a worthier sacrifice for the spirit of her who gave me birth, and who may perhaps, in her liberated and happy state, still know what passes here below. I would desire that my own heart, and the hearts of all that hear me, might bow more completely in obedience to that God and Saviour in whom she trusted, that we may all earnestly seek and abundantly partake of those heavenly consolations which she enjoyed, and which, like a fountain of living waters, are open to all; whilst Christ exclaims to us, 'Ho! everyone that thirsteth, come ye to the waters; and he that hath no money, come ye, buy and eat: yea, come, buy wine and milk without money and without price. Wherefore do ye spend money for that which is not bread, and your labour for that which satisfieth not? Incline your ear, and come unto me; hear, and your soul shall live; and I will make an ever-lasting covenant with you, even the sure mercies of David (Isaiah lv. 1, 2, 3).'"

THE LAST HOURS OF MRS. LEEVES,

Wife of the Rev. W. Leeves, *Rector of Wrington, in Notes by her eldest Daughter* (Mrs. Elsdale).

"On Monday evening, the 6th of February, 1826, at a quarter before six, I received a most unexpected summons to attend the dying bed of my dear mother. I was enabled to leave at half-past seven the same evening, agitated in spirit, but deriving comfort from my interesting fellow-travellers (two Friends), also going on an errand of sorrow. By coach and chaise, I at length reached, on Tuesday evening, the ever-loved Rectory; but on entering the great gates, all seemed to speak the solemn scene within.

" I did not see my dear mother for above an hour after I arrived (which was at half-past ten). Her condition was very distressing. For sometime I stood by her, sorrowfully beholding her suffering state, before she saw me; her first salutation was, 'May God Almighty bless your filial haste, my sweet child!' Her words were warm with affection and gratitude to us all. I continued near her during the night; she spoke little, and happily dozed much.

"Wednesday, Feb. 8th. From midday, after great suffering, my dear parent seemed to be declining. She told us with evident satisfaction, that she felt weaker; her desire to depart was most fervent and astonishing. Had she not possessed a humble yet *assured* hope of bliss, she *could* not have thus smiled at the prospect of death. Though her pains of body were, as her doctor said, such as he had *never* seen surpassed, yet the general bent of her mind was decidedly not to escape from these, but longings to be for ever with her 'beautiful Saviour.' At night, as I leant over her pillow, her countenance brightened, and she exclaimed, 'How shall I mount up?—how *will* it be, the separation of the soul from the body?' I said, 'My dear mother, we are not allowed the vision and understanding of these things here; 'now, we see through a glass darkly, but then face to face.'' 'Oh,' she replied, '*then* how lovely! Oh! for a brighter foretaste of bliss! Tell dear sweet Mrs. Nutcombe that I did not pray so much for a release from my sufferings, as for patience under them.'

" We had prayers round her bed this morning, which were deeply affecting to my father, and to us all ; her enjoyment and animation of soul were truly delightful to witness. The same day, when a text was repeated to her, her looks were most happy, and she said, 'Oh! that is best ; speak as much of these things as possible. My beautiful God, I long to be with Him.' Some words she spoke to me about eleven o'clock this night, were also highly indicative of a happy and blessed state. She was clearly alive to every bodily and mental feeling ; her sufferings seemed bitter, and I wished to be satisfied whether they proceeded *entirely* from the body. I said, 'Your *bodily* distresses are very trying, I hope earnestly your *mind* is at peace?' 'Oh, my dear,' she replied, 'I *think* I have no painful feelings about my God, my *merciful* God ;' and looking anxiously in my face, said, 'do you think I have?' I replied, 'I had the best hope she had not ; for in her intervals of ease more especially, I had rejoiced in her animated longings after the presence of her Saviour.' She was pleased, saying, 'I'm glad you think so.' ' But, my dear mother, the best and happiest, in their heavenly prospects, have dark moments.' 'Oh,' she replied, ' but I call not this a dark moment; I long for my God, *all* the flesh !' Her bright countenance showed, I think, the soul's peace more delightfully than her words.

" About this time, she called her dear son William to her, and spoke most affectionately to him, commending his father to his especial attention. The exertion was too much for her, and caused a paroxysm of pain, which was heart-rending to witness. For many minutes she suffered intensely ; but, blessed be God, it was soon assuaged, and did not return, and she experienced rest for nearly three hours; stillness and peace prevailed, and our hearts were lightened in our sorrows when we contemplated the heavenly-mindedness of our suffering parent.

"Thursday morning, the 9th. My dear mother had an interesting conversation with me about my dear sister. Never shall I forget the beautiful brightness of her countenance, and the eagerness with which she took my hand, and drew me close to her, whilst she spoke of a daughter so deservedly dear to her. During the morning she was tolerably easy, and enjoyed a sweet sleep for two hours. Upon awaking, she looked around, and called for my father and sister. I was near her; she kissed us all, and said, 'I am weaker; you wont have me with you long. I have had a *bright vision;* and though I do not *deserve* heaven, yet I hope to get there.' Her countenance during this most affecting, but sweetly consoling confession, expressed unutterable things, and an unearthly radiance seemed to beam upon her features. My father remarked, 'Nobody deserved heaven, but that it was far better as a favour.' 'Oh,' she replied, with a look most expressive of united joy and humility, 'what a wonderful gift; how far more than I deserve!'

"Her distress of body between the intervals of dozing was very great. In one of these times of trial, she exclaimed, but not with impatience, 'What is death, that I *cannot* pass out of this life?' (Oh! what a sufferer! and what wrestling in prayer, and striving for patience!) Love and kindness, and thoughtfulness for all around her, marked her words and conduct throughout this bitter trial; her 'merciful God and Saviour' being often called upon in her distress.

"After sleeping, she often gazed around in disappointment to find herself still in this vale of sorrow, and not yet with her dear Lord. 'Is it possible I can be yet here!' she would frequently exclaim.

"About four in the morning she seemed to be sinking, and said without dismay, 'The cold hand of death is upon me.' A paroxysm of suffering ensued; after which, she looked at me with calmness, saying, 'Put your hand on my pain, and let me sleep in Jesus.' From eleven o'clock, she slept sweetly for three hours. Her medical attendant told us he thought she could not last till morning, and might be gone in an hour, so we watched our dear charge with trembling solicitude.

"Friday, 10th. At four o'clock, on Friday morning, the whole family assembled around her apparently dying bed. It was a solemn scene, but still a delightful one; the little she spoke was the language of warning, of submission, and of love. She was perfectly conscious of all that passed around her, and noticed all who came to see her. Till about eight o'clock in the evening she remained in a deep and death-like slumber, when she awoke, and blessed God for His great love and mercy towards her, and earnestly expressed her desire to depart to be with her Saviour.

"At this time an interesting scene took place between my dear father and mother, which was overpowering to both, and to all present. My father, with looks of sorrowing love and tenderness, requested that the wedding ring which had for forty years united them so faithfully and happily, should be transferred to *his* finger, where he declared his resolution it should remain. in life and in death. My dear mother instantly complied, looking very sweetly and even playfully, as she placed the ring on my father's finger, saying, 'You have married me, now I will marry you.' This passing revival of our dear parent appeared to us wonderful.

"During the morning, at intervals, my dear mother was tolerably easy; and in one of these gracious seasons, she much enjoyed the sweet fresh air. It was a lovely day; she desired her window to be thrown open, washed her head and face, and sat up in bed some time, and seemed much refreshed. I said, 'The sight of your pretty garden does not make you long to get back to it again?' 'Oh no!' she exclaimed, with a happy smile of inexpressible brightness. I ventured to suggest that the *delay* of her departure *might* be necessary for the trial of her patience. She instantly acceded to the idea, and seemed afterwards more in prayer for this divine grace. She would sometimes exclaim,

'Not one pain too much,—all mercy!' During the night she dozed repeatedly, and once, on awaking to her suffering state, she implored with uplifted hands her Saviour to have pity on her, and receive her to Himself. 'My sufferings are dreadful!' she exclaimed; but checking herself, she sweetly said, with a look of composure, 'I bow with *low* submission, with *low* submission; Thy will be done, O Lord.' This was a solemn, but blessed moment; and from that time my beloved mother evinced increasing resignation to whatever appeared to be the will of God concerning her.

"I was up during the chief part of the night with my mother, at intervals reading some portions of Scripture to her, and having prayers together. Such exercises were, as she could bear them, always delightful to her; and she was always grateful to us for embracing any favourable opportunity for that purpose. At times, when ministering to her necessities, she would call me her 'universal comforter;' and I often experienced how much 'better is the house of mourning than the house of feasting.'

"Saturday, the 11th. Pain, sad pain; again reviving. But let us trust our God that 'all is mercy' with our dear sufferer. She was gently placed upon the couch, and we sat by her in turns, reading from the Olney Hymns the 57th, 1st book, beginning, 'How sweet the name of Jesus sounds.' She enjoyed it truly, and said with warmth, 'Reserve that for my departing spirit.'

"About twelve o'clock in the night, after joining most fervently in prayer and praise, and entreating never to be denied the sweet comfort it afforded, I took her some tea. 'Oh!' she said, 'If I could drink this, and go to my gracious Father: but such a delight is too much to expect.' 'But, my dear mother, you *do* look forward to the joys of heaven; you *are* filled with a bright expectation?' 'Oh! that I am!' she exclaimed, with a radiant smile,—'songs, hymns of praise, harps, psalteries, lutes, dulcimers, and choruses of delight!—oh! too much for such an unworthy creature, the sudden rush of joy which bursts upon the

departing spirit!' I said, 'I think this affliction has been
sanctified and blessed to you, my dear mother; you used to be
timid in respect to the assurance of hope.' 'Oh, but I am not
now; I *fear* not, but *humbly* hope. To morrow is sweet Sunday,
my dear child; and if I *should* then, on that loved morning,
meet with such bliss! I cannot but feel a hope it may be so.'
Soon after this, she seemed to be in delightful thought, her
countenance bright and peaceful; and presently I could hear
her, in a low voice, saying, 'We wait, and wait, from day to day,
and at last the joy comes!'

"Sunday, the 12th. The sweet Sabbath she looked forward
to arrived; and blessed be the God of mercy, it was a day of
calm and consolation to us all. Our beloved parent was much
easier, insomuch that my sister and I took it in turns to attend
divine service. When I returned in the morning, I found her
asleep. She had been in a peculiarly happy and animated
frame of mind; and when she heard the Psalm for the morning
was the 84th, she immediately began singing it, and went
through the first verse with a firm and strong voice, and would
have proceeded, had my sister suffered her. It was one of her
favourite psalms,—one that she had often sung with us all in
sweet harmony.

"In this afflicting state of things our dear father (though
mercifully supported) was relieved of his ministerial duties by
his kind and pious young friend, Mr. Valpy, who, at my mother's
request, visited her after the church service. He spoke and
prayed sweetly with her, and she begged he would soon come
again. She was all humility, and spoke of her own sufferings
as less than she deserved, and as *nothing* compared with the
complex agonies of her beloved Saviour. Her great fear was
that she should appear impatient, and in her moments of pain
express herself in an unsubmissive manner.

"Monday, the 13th. After a night of much merciful relief,
our dear sufferer awoke in dreadful agonies, and prayed fervently
for ease and patience. She soon after fell into a beautiful sleep.
I watched long by her bedside, and felt myself powerfully

supported; I experienced, by the mercy of God that 'profitable is the season of mourning.'

"About three o'clock, my dear father and sister were with me anxiously watching her, believing that she was passing peacefully out of this life; but again she awoke, and beaming with love and kindness, she called us all by name, saying sweetly, 'How kind you are to me! Oh! it is too much, far more than an unworthy creature deserves.' We were deeply affected: the sudden transition from the stillness and solemnity of apparently approaching death, to the bright kindling eye of love, and the words of grateful affection, was unspeakably touching; a moment never to be forgotten. I said, 'My dear mother, we thought we should never have had the happiness of speaking with you again here below.' Her countenance was radiant, and she smiled and replied, 'I did not know I was still in this world.' Her sweet composure bespoke happiness and peace, and she said, 'I think I feel no pain.' The evening was a lovely one; we opened the window, and supporting our dear parent, she enjoyed the fresh air, and said, 'Now let me enjoy the beautiful works of my God *once more !*'—and this was the last she did ever behold them on earth. She was much refreshed, but immediately again wished for quiet and rest saying, as she fell back upon her pillow, 'Let me enjoy myself;' suggesting the thought that she might, in these tranquil periods, be favoured with nearer views of that blessed world she was so ardently panting after. But it is not for us to lift the veil *here;* we 'live by faith, and not by sight.'

"During the evening, our dear parent dozed chiefly. Mr. James (her medical attendant) saw her about nine o'clock. He thought her countenance much altered, and her speech not so clear; but every faculty was alive. He expressed a hope that she might have a more comfortable night. She looked upwards, and said, 'Heaven, heaven!' adding, 'but I do not expect that;' meaning, that she scarcely dared hope to be so blessed *that* night. But I rejoined, 'Perhaps, dear mother, Mr. James does not understand you quite; I am sure you humbly expect heaven?'

'To be sure I do, my child;' and looking expressively at Mr. James, added, 'you do not think me such an infidel!' He assured her that he perfectly understood her, and took leave of her for the last time. It was a blessed night, to see her free from all pain, and calmly awaiting her Lord's call. My father read to her a hymn he had just composed, 'The True Christian's Death.' She lent her attention with looks of affectionate interest, her languid eye bespeaking pleasure; but it was only the last line that seemed to strike her forcibly, and this she repeated over and over again with ardour. She then expressed a wish for prayer; but appearing spent, and inclined to doze, we thought it better to encourage quiet.

" About twelve o'clock, another sad attack of pain came on, and I was aroused from my sleep in the adjoining room by afflicting cries from our dear sufferer of 'torture! torture!' By the mercy of God, her bitter pains were at length allayed, and about two o'clock on Tuesday morning she fell into a sweet sleep. It was an anxious day, as we were expecting every hour the last solemn change.

" At half-past nine in the evening, I had just left my mother's room, but was quickly recalled by her altered breathing: it was evident that the last struggle was at hand. We sent for our dear father, and all fell on our knees to commend the dear departing spirit into the hands of Him who gave it. . . . I listened for her breathing; but all was hushed! The soul was no longer an inhabitant of the body, but had fled into the presence of her Saviour.

"After the first impulses of grief had subsided, her sorrowing partner and his children together knelt down and lifted up their hearts to God in consoling and assuring hope of a sweet reunion before the throne of grace.

" February 14th, 1826."

Letter from J. E. WALTERS, ESQ.

         Ewell, Oct. 26th, 1872.

My dear Mrs. Moon,

I have great pleasure in sending you a copy of the lines which your Grandfather composed and read to your Grandmother when on her deathbed.

In his last letter to me, dated from Bath, 2nd of April, 1828, he spoke of himself as follows :

"I am going home to-morrow, certainly better than when I came here, but I hope sufficiently aware that old ruins are only to be cured by dissolution. Happy for us when the materials can be turned to good account."

This is an interesting little bit, which I thought you would like to have. . . . .

    With kind regards to Dr. Moon,

        I remain,

           Yours truly,

             J. E. WALTERS.

THE TRUE CHRISTIAN'S DEATH,

By the REV. WILLIAM LEEVES, *when his beloved Wife was on her deathbed, Feb.* 1826.

Deceived by fancy's airy breath,
   The false professor fondly errs ;
Covets a proud, triumphant death,
   And thus Divine rebuke incurs.

No better he, whose wand'ring mind
   A full-assured salvation waits ;
Or, urged by force, expects to find
   His way to the celestial gates.

Errors like these debase the soul,
 And cheat her into noxious ways ;
The sweets of humbleness control,
 And wrong, the form of right portrays.

Our genuine Christian, on her God
 Most humbly stays with true delight ;
Through hope, content to kiss the rod,
 And rather trusts to faith than sight.

Does agonizing pain assail,
 And the fell fiend distrust suggest,
Her actual lot she may bewail,
 But bows to the Divine behest.

Convinced that God's supremely just,
 With calmness she supports her pain ;
Trusts, when the frame is turned to dust,
 Her soul shall with her Saviour reign.

No merits of her own she pleads,
 Her expectation's from above ;
And, sensible of past misdeeds,
 Relies on *Christ's* redeeming *blood.*

LINES

BY THE

REV. WILLIAM LEEVES.

(A few, written by his friends, have their names attached).

TO A LADY PLAYING THE VIOLIN.

(Miss Wathen, afterwards Mrs. Leeves).

Whene'er you touch the trembling string,
   Whose unison you sweetly sound,
The notes involuntary ring,
   And *sounds* the power of *sense* confound.

So may our hearts, my gentle maid,
   In sympathetic tones unite ;
Should *yours* in pleasure's lap be laid,
   May *mine*, responsive feel delight !

Or should affliction's storm descend,
   And nip you with its cruel blast,
May I, your shelter and your friend,
   Protect and aid you to the last.

May kindred melodies conspire
   To sweeten the duet of life,
And banish far discordant ire,
   The parent and the food of strife,

THE HAPPY TRIO.

Mrs. Leeves (Anna, or Anne), daughter of Dr. Wathen, was celebrated for her skilful performance upon the violin. Mrs. Eckersall, her
sister, had a remarkably fine voice, and the Rev. W. Leeves played the
violoncello with skill. The following lines were sent to Dr. Wathen upon
the occasion of this Trio departing from London for Guildford.
The lines were found among Mr. Leeves' MS. papers, in a letter
directed to Dr. Wathen, without signature.

What gone, sweet harmonists! Then Taste, adieu!
No more those pleasing airs shall charm the ear:
Fair Katherine's warble,—graceful Anna's bow,
Which tuned to harmony the soul: no more
The enraptured multitude shall scale the walls
To catch, from thy sweet lips, one note divine ;
Lament, harmonic Vento!—Sossor, weep!—
And tuneful Hayes, deplore your honours fled!
Unrivall'd now, Miss Sermen, draw your bow,
And Kistorini, venture to come forth
And charm the sense, nor dread a rival song!
Thrice happy Guildford! didst thou know the bliss
That soon awaits thee! Rosin all the bows
That can within thy spacious walls be found ;
Your fiddle-strings prepare, of Roman gut ;
Your grumbling basses, hautboys, pipes, and tabors ;
And march, with jocund step, to meet
The Happy Trio!

SONG.

Found among the Rev. W. Leeves' MS. papers (without signature).

Ye powers, who taught my artless sighs
  A kindred heart to gain,
Teach me that blessing still to prize,
  And as I prize, maintain.

E

Let kind attention, pleasing care,
  O'er all my thoughts preside ;
Let love in every glance appear,
  And every action guide.

If e'er a cloud of peevish spleen
  Our brighter hours o'ercast,
Let fancy quickly shift the scene
  To fond endearments past.
O'er every joy our breasts have felt
  Let faithful memory rove ;
And teach the hard'ning heart to melt
  With recollected love.

Thus every flower that form'd the wreath
  Of Hymen's festive chain,
Uninjured fragrance still shall breathe,
  And every charm retain.
Thus, while our hearts delighted prove
  Our envied bliss secure,
We'll boast the joys of wedded love
  As permanent as pure.

ON THE DEATH OF " PRINCE."

(The Dog.)

1815.

Princes too often fill the world with tears,
But then, 'tis by exciting anxious fears ;
The Prince *we've* lost ne'er forged oppression's chain,
To follow others seemed *his* greatest gain.

By most regretted, and by all admired,
Such *private* grief few Princes have inspired ;
For seldom can the page of history trace
Domestic feelings for a *Royal race.*

THE FLOWERS.

Translation from the French (without signature).

With each expanding flower we find
Some pleasing sentiment combined :
Love in the myrtle bloom is seen,
Remembrance to the violet clings ;
Peace brightens in the olive's green,
Hope from the half-closed iris springs ;
And *victory* on the laurel grows,
And *woman* blushes in the rose !

TO MISS VALPY.

(Daughter of the celebrated Grammarian and Scholar, DR. VALPY.)

1815.

Of all the pies you can behold,
Of fruit or meat, or hot or cold,
Molland herself has never sold
   One equal to a—Val-py.

The outward crust so soft and fair,   `
The inward fruit so sweet and rare ;
There's none on earth can sure compare
   Their pastry with a—Val-py.

Or if you wish a season'd treat,
To render your repast complete,
There's learning's bone affords the meat,
   When pick'd out of a—Val-py.

Greece has no sauce of greater fame,
The Attic salt no more you'll name ;
Of this be cautious, how you aim
   E'er to *cat up* a—Val-py.

E 2

TO THE MISSES WYLDE.

(One of whom married a son of Dr. Valpy.)

1815.

Though the raspberry and currant of each tart the zest is,
Yet the lovers of nature think *Wylde* fruit the best is.

ON MR. HENRY LEEVES.

(Afterwards the Rev. Henry Leeves), by Mrs. Toriano,
Weston-super-Mare.

Dirt, and the youth I sing, whose matchless art
Without the aid of wheelbarrow or cart,
Could sand remove, or neatly cover mire ;
Could turf o'er stones, and trim the twig and brier ;
Banish the hardships of a tedious lane,
And make each rugged footstep smooth and plain ;
How shall the grateful Muse, in numbers meet,
Extol the work so useful, so complete ?
Not Hercules himself, defying danger,
More skilfully cleansed stable, rack, and manger ;
For what were all the filth of hoof and horn,
To stain of blackberry, or scratch of thorn ?
Then loud, O youth, thy praises shall resound,
Whilst ladies of their dress be careful found ;
Whilst each a cap, pelisse, and bonnet wears,
Whilst lace and riband hitch, and muslin tears ;
Whilst curls grow straight, exposed to evening dew,
And shoes and stockings can be wetted through.
Whilst Weston's sea shall boast the rising wave,
And Anchor-head invite the fair to lave ;

Whilst foaming kettles boil, and rocks shall sigh,
And kelp and seaweed in confusion lie ;
Whilst, *Leeves*, thy cottage* shall adorn the scene,—
All taste without, all harmony within.

ON THE DEATH OF TWO
GRANDCHILDREN.

(Children of MRS. E.)

1815.

Be still, ye common griefs ! to this give way,—
Two lovely children lost in one sad day !
The first, parental aid scarce lays to rest,
Another falls ! Nor judge e'en this behest
A lot too hard : behold their angels rise
On wings of innocence, and flit the skies !
Think on a change so blest, and wipe your streaming eyes.

ON THE DEATH OF A THIRD
GRANDCHILD.

(Soon after the preceding.)

That bell again " flings to the hollow gale
Its sullen sound,"—another child to wail !
The first,—while pleasing recollection plays
O'er each remembrance of her winning ways,—
To undermine sweet resignation's base essays.

---

* The cottage here referred to, which MR. LEEVES built, was the
first gentleman's house in Weston. A section of it still remains at the
end of the Esplanade, and goes by the name of "Leeves' Cottage."

This fresh avulsion calls for all our tears :
A rip'ning intellect, with rip'ning years,
Seems to elicit every fond regard,—
Of temporal fame to promise the reward,—
And thus from dark regret the mind refuse to guard.

But hear the voice of heaven ; short-sighted man
In vain his real good attempts to scan.
Look to the early profligate, whose way
Embitters each parental night and day ;
The trifling idler,—desultory wight,—
Whose self-applause creates his chief delight,
Who follows fashion's shade till vice obscures his sight.

How canst thou tell, with all thy fost'ring care,
But some seducer might thine empire share ?
The world's a system full of dang'rous flaws,
Both Scylla and Charybdis ope their jaws,—
'Tis hard to trace its paths, yet keep God's righteous laws.

Ye loving Parents, hush your tender cries,
Behold your angels floating in the skies !
Of this you may be certain and secure.
For this, who would not any loss endure,
And selfish thoughts resign, to make their bliss so sure ?

LINES

BY THE

REV. W. LISLE BOWLES,

ON FIRST HEARING *MISS STEPHENS*

(Afterwards COUNTESS OF ESSEX)

SING "AULD ROBIN GRAY."

Oh ! when I hear thee sing of " Jamie far away,"
" Of faither and of mither," and of " Auld Robin Gray,"
I listen till I think it is Jeany's self I hear,
" And I look in thy face,"* with a blessing and a tear.

I look in thy face, for my heart it is not cold,
Though winter's frost is stealing on, and I am growing old ;
Those tones I shall remember as long as here I live,
And the blessing and the tear shall be the thanks I give.

The tear it is for summers that so blithesome have been,
For the flowers that all are faded, and "the days that I have seen;"
The *blessing* is for thee, lassie : mayst thou still rejoice,
Though tenderness is on thy look, and pity in thy voice.

The blessing is for thee, whose song, so sadly sweet,
Recalls the music of " Lang Syne " to which my heart has beat ;
Oh ! may the days that shine to thee still happiness prolong,
And every sorrow of the heart be ended with thy song !

" Such is national prejudice, that many well-informed Scotch people
contend that this exquisite Melody is originally Scotch, though the author is
yet living and well-known,—the REV. WILLIAM LEEVES, Rector of Wrington,
in Somersetshire."—*Derby Mercury*, April, 1823.

---

* " She look'd in my face till my heart was like to break."
This line MISS STEPHENS gives with exquisite pathos.

"AULD ROBIN GRAY"
SUPPLEMENTED.

By Lady E. Lindsay (afterwards Countess of Hardwicke, MS.)

The spring it was past, it was summer nae mair,
And thinly were scatter'd the leaves in the air ;
" Oh winter," says Jeany, " we kindly agree,
" For the sun he looks *wae* when he shines upon me."
Nae longer she *grat*, for her tears were a' spent,
Despair it was come, and she thought it content ;
She thought it content, but her cheek it grew pale,
And she droop'd like the snow-drop cut down by the hail.

Her mither was vex'd, and her faither was wae,
" What ails you, my bairn ?" they would oftentimes say ;
" Your wheel you turn round, and you come little speed.
" Your hand it grows feeble, and weak is your tread."
She smiled when she heard them, to banish their fear,
But sad looks the smile that is seen through a tear ;
And bitter the tear which is forced by a love
Which reason and honour can never approve.

Her faither was vexed, and her mither was wae,
But dowie and silent sat Auld Robin Gray ;
He spake not a word, but his cheek it grew lean,
Like the side of a brae where the torrent had been.
Nae question he ask'd her concerning her health,
He look'd at her often, and aye ! 'twas by stealth ;
Then his heart it grew full, and often he feign'd
To gang to the door to see if it rain'd.

Then he took to his bed, nae physic he sought,
He ordered his neighbours around to be brought ;
While Jeany supported his head in its place,
His tears trickled down, and fell on his face.

" Oh, kill me not Jeany," said Auld Robin Gray,
" I have not deserved this, I've something to say :
" I knew not, dear Jeany, I knew not your vow,
" In mercy forgive me,—' twas *I* stole the cow !

" I valued not Crummie, I thought but of thee,
" I thought it was *her* stood between you and me ;
" While *she* fed your parents, ah ! *did nae ye say*
" Ye never *wad* marry *that Auld Robin Gray !* "

ON A DAUGHTER BECOMING BLIND.

Lines written by MR. WILLIAMS (a friend of the REV. W. LEEVES) on
seeing the last flower of his Daughter's painting, after she had become blind.

Here, hapless maid ! here end thy playful pains,
  Nature hath shut the book,—thy task is done ;
Of all her various charms, what now remains ? —
  To smell the violet, and feel the sun.

In liberal toil thy youthful hands did grow,
  Quick moving at thy better sense's call ;
That better sense is gone !—their task is now
  To twist the yarn, or grope the friendly wall.

Oh fate severe !—earth's lesson early taught,
  That all is vain save virtue, love, and truth ;
We own it, all that through life's day have wrought,
  But thou hast learnt it in the morn of youth.

Pupil of heaven thou art !—compute thy gain,
  When dulness loads thee, or regret assails ;
All is not lost, for Faith and Hope remain,
  And gentle Charity, which never fails.

How love shall glow where envy might have burn'd !—
Now every hand and every eye is thine ;
Each human form, each object undiscern'd,
From borrow'd organs thou shall still divine.

But thy great Maker's own transcendent light,
His love ineffable, His ways of old,
His perfect wisdom, and His presence bright,
" *Thine* eyes, and not another's, shall behold."

ON THE MARRIAGE OF A NIECE.

Lines written by Miss MARIANNE WATHEN on the marriage of Miss
HARRIET ECKERSALL * with MR. MALTHUS, the celebrated writer on
" Population."

' Twas at the op'ning of the vernal year,
When violets and primroses appear,
And from her bounteous lap Spring lavish throws
Each lovely flower that wept ' neath Winter's snows ;
When morning purpled in the glowing east,
And Sol with radiance all the meadows drest,
Forth from his rosy bower in the grove,
With hasty step advanced the god of love :
" Awake ! my little troop of smiling loves,
" Prepare my car, put to my fleetest doves ;
" We're bidden to the marriage of a pair
" Who long have been my most peculiar care :
" Ere burning noon assumes his sultry pride,
" We must away to meet the charming bride."
He spoke, and graceful waved his little hand,
The doves obey the imperial Boy's command,
Who thus resumes,—" Yes, 'tis well worth our while

---

* The Ladies here mentioned were both Nieces of the REV. W. LEEVES.

" To gladden this fair wedding with a smile ;
" Endow'd with sense, with truth, with polish'd air,
" And with a manly heart to guard the fair,
" The youth,—no flutt'ring coxcomb of the day,
" Who laughs at mine and Hymen's gentle sway.
" The maid,—unlike the light coquettish dame
" Of fashion, who disclaims all but the name
" Of wife,—is soft and gentle as the dove,
" The pride of virtue, and the pride of love.
" Sweet temper fills her breast, illumes her eye,
" And on her lip hangs fair sincerity ;
" Health's vernal tints her modest cheeks adorn
" With all the beauty of the blushing morn.
" For such as these, my torch burns bright and pure,
" And shall to life's last hour so endure.
" Yes," cried the God, " each year shall, on its wing
" Unfading and substantial pleasures bring ;
" And when, at length, Age sheds his silvery snows
" Upon their heads, and when no longer glows
" Their frame with smiling youth's ethereal fire,
" Yet in their hearts my flame shall not expire :
" Bless'd in each other's virtues, then well-tried,
" Each other's dearest blessing, comfort, pride
" They shall remain ; and when their course is run,
" And set in death is life's once-glorious sun,
" Hand locked in hand, they both shall wing their way
" To blissful regions of eternal day !"

ON ATTAINING THE FULL AGE
OF MAN

70 ætat. June 11th, 1819.

Hail, awful season ! when the book of God
Declares the term of human life to close ;
When all its relishes are said to end,
And the dark mountains open to our view.
This morn completes th' important term ; but where,
Where are those indications of decay
Which numbers feel ?—where is that waste of body,
Or, what is worse, that infancy of mind
So frightful at the close of earthly days ?

I thank my God, through Jesus Christ our Lord,
That it hath pleased him to prolong my course,
And to protect me from those ills in age   .
Which some have to lament in early youth.
Health, mod'rate strength, an even tranquil mind,
Domestic happiness in full extent,
But that my second self re-stricken lies.
(May piety suggest it for the best :
Submission will enhance the sacrifice,
And calmly bow to the Divine behest
What'er it be a kind Creator wills :
Her sharpest sting affliction points in vain,
When endless joys approach so near to view.)

Such is my favour'd portion,—an employ
That kings, in ancient times, have aim'd to grace,
And for its work's sake claims to be esteem'd ;—
Such is the bounty of our great Preserver !

That all my good be not exhausted here,
And evil things in future life succeed,
May heav'nly grace assist me to discharge
Those duties which a righteous God demands ;
Or may His mercy pardon the omission   ˙
Through the atonement of His blessed Son !

Bridge Engraver: Wright ...

[*On an attack of Illness two days later.*]

Sunday, June 13.

Awful event! that nature's right so soon
Should be exerted. Though th' attack be slight
Which heav'nly mercy sends, still 'tis enough
To teach the vain fragility of man,
And that we know not what a day may bring.
To be prepared, whene'er our Lord shall call,
Affords the only harbinger of peace.
Religion with her calm, resign'd delights,
Though the peculiar food of elder life,
In ev'ry stage will nourish and support,
And point the peaceful path to endless bliss.

THE SIGHING ROCK.

1821.

At Weston-super-Mare, some distance up the hill, there is a ledge or craggy Rocks. From a small hole in one of them, the air issuing produces a sound like *tremendous sighs!* Near here, through a circular perpendicular passage in a rock, the sea rushes up, and boils over in foaming spray. The writer supposes the Sighing Rock, with "o'erflowing briny tears," to be a Youth turned into stone.

The following verses refer to these Rocks, which MR. LEEVES called " The Sighing Rock and the Boiling Kettle."

On Somerset's delightsome coast
    Where Bristol's Channel flows,
Nature a ledge of rocks can boast
    Which scarce a rival knows.
Here once a fated youth repair'd,
    His doleful tale to sigh ;
The precipice he wildly dared,
    Nor deemed his end so nigh.

When thus the Genius of the shore
  Address'd the mournful youth :—
" Thy pains are ended ; thou no more
  Shalt urge thy slighted truth.
In pity of thy plaintive moan,
  Thy painful pangs and throes,
That wasted form shall turn to stone,
  Which pain nor torment knows.

The village swains resorting here,
  These rugged cliffs to dare,
Deep hollow sighs shall fill with fear,
  Lest they, too, brave the fair.
Thy briny tears shall bubbling rise,
  In rocky cavern pent,
An emblem of o'erflowing eyes
  For time in love misspent."

May youthful lovers warning take
  From this disastrous tale,
Lest their own misery they make
  When lost engagements fail !
Let nymphs beware !—a stony heart
  May swains to stone transform ;
And swains act well the lover's part,
  Such frigid hearts to warm.

BY S. I. A.

On giving a Crown at a Bazaar, at Wrington, for a Pair of Garters knit by
MRS. HANNAH MORE.

About 1822.

A Royal Garter is a prize
  Which even kings are proud to own ;
But made by one so kind and wise, ·
  This pair is more than worth a *crown*.

THE BURTHEN OF BRIGHTON DONKEYS.

About 1810.   Found among the MSS. (without signature).

The Donkeys of Brighton are alternately employed by *belles* and *smugglers* :—They carry *angels* by day, and *spirits* by night.

IMPROMPTU.

By the REV. J. WHARTON, on several Ladies being given as Toasts,
all of whose names began with the letter B.

How strange, we cry, of fortune the decree,
That all our favourites should begin with B !
But soon is solved this parodox of ours,
The *Bee* lights always on the sweetest flowers !

HYMN.

Father of Lights, Almighty Lord !
Thy praise we chant with one accord ;
Like incense let our hymn ascend
To Thee, our Saviour, Guide, and Friend.

Let not distraction's cloud opaque
Our frail addresses sinful make ;
But let the brightness of Thy face
Cheer ev'ry heart, fill ev'ry space.

Bless'd breezes then our bark shall guide,
Joy sitting by religion's side ;
And, humble Prayer (be thou but near)
Shall to celestial havens steer.

By Thee protected, we shall sail
Through troubled seas with prosp'rous gale ;
The pilot, Hope, direct our way,
And stem the wave of cold delay.

ON PSALM XC.

1822.

O God, Thou wast in power sublime,
Before the mortal birth of time ;
E'er earth her flow'ry lap had spread,
Or mountains rear'd their tow'ring head.
At thy displeasure lordly man
Contracts his being to a span ;
Closes his transitory day
And passes like a dream away.

At morn he glows with healthy bloom,
At evening drops into the tomb ;
As fades, upon the river's side,
The verdant meadow's grassy pride.
Oh ! then, ere youth be pass'd away,
Prepare us for the mortal day ;
Our minds with heav'nly grace supply,
And fit us every hour to die.

WHITSUNDAY.·

Found in the REV. W. LEEVES' hand-writing (without signature).
April 30th, 1822.

Come, Holy Spirit, heavenly guest,
And fill with light my darken'd breast ;
A sense of sacred truth inspire,
My languid bosom touch with fire ;
And make me, when in prayer I kneel,
To glow with apostolic zeal.

Come, Holy Spirit, and expel
The foe that drives me to rebel ;
The tumults of temptation still,
O'ermaster my presumptuous will ;
And shew me, by thy secret aid,
The paths of duty easy made.

Come, Holy Spirit, calm within
The wild inquietude of sin ;
And to my heart,—my alter'd heart,—
Thy peace and heavenly love impart ;
And when from sin and sorrow free,
Make it a temple worthy Thee.

Come, Holy Spirit, here below,
Thy sanctifying grace bestow ;
Guide me through life, and when I die,
And in the grave forgotten lie,
Again Thy mighty power display,
And raise me at the judgment-day.

Wrington.

ON HIS 77TH BIRTHDAY.

June 11th, 1825.

God of my life ! what praise is due
    To Thee who, true in all Thy ways,
Still deign'st my being to renew
    Beyond the bourn of mortal days !

    Mindful of every past event
    Which through Thy grace, has marked my way,
May I contemplate these as sent
    In mercy, from the God of day !

F

Few, I believe, can calmly view
  A retrospect so free from pain ;
Domestic comfort, more than due,
  Has aim'd its blessings to maintain.

Let those who sweetly now conspire
  To smooth my earthly pillow's down,
Accept the grateful fond desire
  That happiness their path may crown.

Precarious is the worn-out thread
  Which, ere 'tis cut, is apt to fail ;
May I, till number'd with the dead,
  In bark of perseverance sail.

May I and mine acceptance find
  With God, for a Redeemer's sake ;
And true to Him, in heart and mind,
  A blest society partake !

Rectory, Wrington.

ON HIS 78TH BIRTHDAY.

1826.

[*" On entering my 78th year,"* original heading.]

Transcendent Ruler of our ways,
Thy mercy has prolong'd my days
Beyond the short and fragile span
Thou hast allotted here to man.
Since *this,* seven years have roll'd away,
Yet on this earth I longer stay,
Blest with a share of health and power
Demanding praise at every hour.
Bereft, indeed, of her whose love
(A prudent wife is from above),

Whose sweet affection fills a heart
From which it never can depart ;
Whose fond remembrance shall endure
Till hope a heavenly seat ensure.
Blest also with deserving ties
From whence the seeds of love arise,
A son,* whose honest nature flows,
And kindly sheds on all he knows :—
Another † who, in foreign lands,
Puts forth God's Word with pious hands :—
Another ‡ who, on distant shores,
With grief affection's bar deplores :—
A daughter ‖ who, as wife and mother,
Can scarce be match'd with such another ;
Whose charity to all extends,
And ranks the wretched as her friends :—
Another § who, beyond all praise,
Now forms the comfort of my days ;
Whose care can every wish prevent,
And, mother-like, ensure content.
From such delightful ties may I detach my heart,
Lord ! that Thy servant may in peace depart.

Rectory, Wrington.

---

* His eldest son, William.　　† His second son, Henry.
‡ His third son, George.　‖ His eldest daughter, Marianne.
§ His youngest daughter, Elizabeth.

F 2

ON HIS 78TH BIRTHDAY.

1826.

[" *Thoughts on the Evening of a Natal Day,*" *original heading.*]

Threescore and eighteen birthdays have gone by,
My glass is quite run out, yet here am I !
I've lived to witness the expiring breath
Of her whose lot was bound with mine till death ;
Whose virtues blest me in this frail abode,
And now have wafted her to rest with God.
May *He* permit her spirit to descend
A guardian angel to her widow'd friend !
And guide to heaven a family she loved,
Who, copying *her*, affectionate have proved ;
Who, whether scions on the parent tree,
Or grafted in some distant clime they be,
The dews of heaven are anxious to receive,
And nature's sad defect, through grace, retrieve.
One branch I fondly hoped, e'er this, t' have seen,
But in his place is sent his *heroine Queen,**
Who, Charity herself, by love, intends
For duty's sacred call to make amends,
And with her budding offspring to supply
The vacuum of a Son who stands so high.
But let us bow to the Divine behest,
Convinced that heaven's decrees are ever best ;·
And if to extend God's Word divides us *now*,
What joys will heavenly intercourse bestow,
Should faith and resignation smooth the way
And join us in the blaze of endless day !
May all my earthly days, like osiers, bend
To the soft breezes which my soul befriend ;

* MRS. H. LEEVES returned alone from Turkey, with three children.

And as the dew revives the fading flow'rs,
May heavenly influence cheer my fleeting hours :
So cheer them, that all dread of death may cease,
And I may say when call'd, " Lord, I depart in peace."

REMINISCENCES.

The following lines were written by the REV. W. LEEVES at the age of
78, in 1826, the year of MRS. LEEVES' death, and referring to their Marriage.

Could sluggish memory require
To call to mind th' extinguish'd fire,
Illumed by one whose gifts might vie
With any wife beneath the sky,
The house in view a tale would tell
Which forty years cannot dispel.
There * 'twas decreed, through friendly aid,
That Hymen's padlock should pervade
Two hearts where sympathy prevail'd,
And since in blissful bark have sail'd.
Regret might now elicit tears,
But consolation's charm appears,
And proves an end so calm, and so resign'd,
Should *raise*, and *not depress*, the feeling mind ;
Should prompt to imitation here below,
That *endless* union from that source may flow.
And when the sweet attentions I survey
With which affection's child† bestrews my way ;
When all th' endearments to my view arise
Which absent love so readily supplies ;
No change can *here* be wished,—the total sum
Is peace and pardon in a world to come.

---

* Written in sight of a house where a Happy Marriage had
formerly been concluded.
†His daughter, MISS E. LEEVES, who lived with him till his death.

78

NOTE AFTER A SONNET

Addressed to the late LADY ANNE BARNARD *(neé* LINDSAY*) on her Ballad of "Auld Robin Gray," by* JOHN TAYLOR, ESQ., *in the* Sun *Newspaper of Sept.* 3, 1825.

"As there have been several reports respecting the music to which this interesting ballad has been sung, it is proper to state that Lady Anne Barnard (*neé* Lindsay) informed the author of the above lines (John Taylor, Esq.) that she wrote it to accord with an old Scotch air, the words of which she did not then know ; but hearing the words some time after, she found them so different from what she expected, that she regretted having adapted her ballad to that air. The music to which the ballad has hitherto been sung, and which is so much admired, was certainly composed by the Rev. Mr. Leeves."

ON CONSTANCY.

Found among the MSS. in MRS. LEEVES' handwriting (without signature).

When kindred hearts together join,
And like the oak and ivy twine,
How blest the happy pair!—
But should the oak receive a wound,
Is not the tendril ivy found
To feel an equal share ?
Such hearts as these in union ever glow,
And, twining, tremble at, or joy or woe.

Written by HENRY LEEVES, ESQ., *on the marriage of his son, the* REV. WILLIAM LEEVES, *with* MISS WATHEN.

(E. LEEVES.)
May 4th, 1786.

May the union of this day be
Happy and prosperous, and lasting as the
Virtues of William and Anna !

(Found among MISS E. LEEVES' MSS.)

LINES

Found in MRS. LEEVES' *workbox, after her death.*

(In her handwriting, without signature).

The great Jehovah hath decreed
That all mankind should die ;
And as the lightning's rapid speed
Our precious moments fly.
This mortal frame will soon decay,
And moulder into dust ;
Lie buried in its native clay,
From pain and labour rest.

My spirit longs to take her flight,
And leave this dark abode,
To mingle with the saints in light,
Before the throne of God.
At thy command, O Lord, let Death
These brittle walls break down ;
And let me soon resign my breath
For an immortal crown.

I long for my celestial home,
To dwell in endless day ;
Oh ! let Elijah's chariot come
And take my soul away,
To join with the triumphant host
Who round the Throne adore
The Father, Son, and Holy Ghost,
In concert evermore.

LINES

By the Rev. W. Leeves, 1826.

Many the blessings shower'd on me,
Thanks, Lord, for which, are due to Thee.
Thy favours manifold exceed
The power of speech, through word or deed.

Unbroken still the thread of life ;
A family devoid of strife ;
A heart that's turned, I trust to God,
Submissive to his gentle rod ;
A child,* whose unremitting care,
Teaches my widow'd heart to bear,
And wait in humble hope to rise
And join my partner in the skies.

All praise eternally be given
By men on earth, and saints in heaven,
To God the Father, and the Son,
And Holy Ghost, the Three in One !

LINES

By Mr. Kemble, *of Bristol, on the* Rev. H. D. Leeves'
sojourn at Constantinople, before going to Athens.

"The Leaves of the Tree were for the healing
of the nations."—Rev. xxii. 2.

An island far north learnt the destitute state
Of a Mediterranean station ;
And in sympathy, knowing their consequent fate,
Sent Leeves to present them salvation.

---

* Miss E. Leeves, who lived with him till his death.

So dark and ensanguined the rigorous views
  Of Mahómet's deluding creation,
'Twas thought they would certainly welcome the news
  Of Leeves, for the healing the nation.

But alas! by enslaving dominion enthrall'd,
  They yield to their full degradation;
Choose the sensual bait, to the treasure of gold
  From Leeves, for the healing their nation.

Their destiny sure will o'ertake them anon,
  For rejecting the proffer'd salvation,
When the ever-green Leeves from the region is gone
  Of this sin-sick destructible nation.

A LETTER

From the REV. H. D. LEEVES, *to the Editor of* THE TIMES.

" Mr. Editor,

" I observed in your paper of Saturday last, a letter on the subject of the authorship of 'Auld Robin Gray,' in which your correspondent claims for my father (the late Rev. Wm. Leeves), the Composition both of the Music and Words of this well-known Ballad. You remark in a note, 'There are so many claimants for this song, that posterity will be sadly puzzled: but that you incline to the opinion which ascribes it to Lady Lindsay.'

" As I have it in my power to set the matter at rest, as far as my father is concerned, I feel it to be my duty (both in justice to his memory, and for the satisfaction of the public, before whom the question has been not unfrequently agitated) to state to you the facts of the case. The Music of this ballad is, then, undoubtedly, my father's composition; but not (so) the Words. He composed the air about the year 1770, at Richmond, where he then resided; and the words were put into his hands by the

Honble. Mrs. Byron, which he understood at that time, and ever afterwards believed to have been (the composition of) written by Lady Anne Lindsay. Copies being handed about in private, the air after some time got into print, without the author's consent, and soon acquired that place in the public favour which it has since maintained: and the world uninformed as to its origin, seem to have set it down as an old Scotch melody.

" My father, little solicitous of notoriety, and content with the approbation of his private friends, for a long time took no measures to claim his undoubted offspring; until at length, at the urgent recommendation of his old and valued friend, the late Mr. Hammersley, of Pall Mall, who was one of those who had known the air in MS., before it got into print, he was induced, in the year 1812, to republish it with his own name, together with a Collection of Sacred Airs, also of his composition, prefixing to the whole a Preface, and an Address to Mr. Hammersley, in which he states the circumstances abovementioned, as well known to that gentleman, and to which, if necessary, he could have borne his testimony.*

" I will only add, that musical composition, chiefly of late on sacred subjects, had been the favourite recreation of my father, to the very close of his life, nearly 50 years of which have been passed in this parish in the exercise of his pastoral duties. Many of these Compositions, known only to his private friends, may perhaps be esteemed not unworthy of the author of the music of ' Auld Robin Gray.'

" I remain, your very obedient Servant,

" H. D. LEEVES.

" Wrington, Somerset,

" July 19, 1828."

---

* This publication has not, however, had a very wide circulation.

"AULD ROBIN GRAY."

(From a Newspaper.)

"In the life of Thomas Moore, by Lord John Russell, occurs the following passage :—
"'Leaves, a clergyman, was the author of the words of 'Auld Robin Gray.' I already knew that Lady Anne Lindsay composed the music.'—*Lord John Russell's Life of Thomas Moore*, vol. 2, p. 180.

"Now the facts of the case are just the reverse. They are as follows, and we have good reason for knowing the truth of them. Lady Anne Lindsay, looking over a volume of ancient Scotch songs, admired an air, 'The bridegroom greets when the sun gangs doun;' the words she did not much like, and wrote her touching ballad, 'Auld Robin Gray,' for adaptation to it. The Hon. Mrs. Byron, a friend of Lady Anne Lindsay, gave these lines to the late Rev. Wm. Leeves (not Leaves), then a young officer of the Guards, afterwards (cedant arma togæ) Rector of Wrington, Somerset, who was uncle to the Rev. C. Eckersall. He (Mr. Leeves) did not know they had been arranged to this old Scotch air, nor did he see it until quite late in life, after he had composed for them his beautiful recitative and air, so often and affectingly sung by the famed 'Kitty Stephens,' now Countess of Essex. The two airs have not the slightest resemblance to each other.

"There are numbers who still imagine the air to be an old Scotch one. Poor Wilson, who used to give such admirable illustrations of Scotch music, used to mention this fact, in one of his delightful entertainments.

"Mr Leeves was the composer of several sacred airs of much merit, which were bound up with the authenticated copy of his popular and most beautiful ballad, and published many years ago. He was rector of the same village (Wrington) in which Hannah More long lived, and with whom he was on

terms of intimacy. He died not many years since in that village,
full of years, sincerely loved and honoured by his numerous
relatives and friends."

LINES

" On seeing an Engraving of the first *English Church erected
amid the ancient city of Athens."* *

"Tomb of the mighty! o'er whose ashes lie
The far-famed ruins of a thousand thrones,
Dark are thy prostrate columns, while a shade
Of countless years indelves their sculptured forms.
I hail thee! Peace is now within thy domes,
That erst re-echoed back the martial strain
Of many a stately triumph; but which now
Point with the warning voice of centuries,
To where thy highest hopes, ambition, fell!
Where stands thy noble Forum? where the stately arch
Through which Pisístratus a triumph led?
The shades of night may mantle all their glories,
But cannot rear one gilded stone again!
Where stood thy fair Pantheon,—noble pile?
Where bowed the Renegade of distant climes,
Now smiles the Temple of the living God!
Mark how serene it rears its humble shrine,—
Yet crowned with chaplets brighter than thy sons'
O mighty Athens! in their proudest lore.
From thy dark ashes, laden with the wealth
A thousand kings were slaughtered to supply,
Built he an altar, lasting as his name!
Now as the glowing sunset lights thy ruins,
See, Athens! it looks on thee, as a mother
Weeps to behold a wayward, ruined child."

* This Church was erected chiefly through the exertions of the REV. H.
D. LEEVES, 1842.

" AN OLD VOLUNTEER MARCH.

" *To the Editor of* THE MIRROR.

"Wrington, Sept. 16, 1861.

" Dear Sir,

" I send you the words of the Volunteer March alluded to in the *Mirror* of last Saturday (page 8), which may do good if inserted in the next.

"Yours truly,   B."

"MARCH VOLUNTEERS!"

"*A War Song and Chorus, inscribed to the Volunteers of the United Kingdom, about* 1802, *by the* REV. WM. LEEVES* *(never before printed)*".

March, Volunteers !
Be patient, firm, and true ;
Your country's liberty
May now depend on you.
 Guard your king, then who's afraid ?
 Guard your laws, then who's afraid ?
 Guard your religion, who's afraid ?
Defend them in the field,
True freemen ne'er to slaves will yield !

March, Volunteers !
Be steady, brave, and bold ;
Protect from violence
Your helpless and your old.

---

* " The REV. WM. LEEVES was the composer of the beautiful melody of ' Auld Robin Gray.' "

Think of your families, who's afraid ?
Think of your comforts, who's afraid ?
Think of your God, then who's afraid ?
Defend them in the field,
True freemen ne'er to slaves will yield !

March, Volunteers !
Your ranks and files well drest ;
Silence and discipline
As soldiers, suit us best.
Trust your commanders, who's afraid ?
Wait for your orders, who's afraid ?
Then rout your enemy, who's afraid ?
And drive them from the field,
For conscript slaves to British freemen sure
    must yield !

A FEW

BRIEF INCIDENTS

IN THE LIFE OF THE

REV. H. D. LEEVES, B.D.

ON THE DEATH OF
THE REV. H. D. LEEVES, B.D.

From THE TIMES, 1845.

"THE LATE REV. HENRY D. LEEVES.—We are much grieved to record the decease, at Beirout, on the 8th ult., of the Rev. Henry D. Leeves, Chaplain to the British Embassy, and minister of the English Episcopal Church at Athens, and for upwards of twenty-five years the zealous and valuable agent of the British and Foreign Bible Society, first at Constantinople, and afterwards at Athens, previously to which he was for three years chaplain to the Factory at Madeira. He may in truth be said to have exiled himself from his native land for the Gospel's sake. The translation of the New Testament into the modern Greek language, and now in use throughout the Greek territory, was accomplished under his immediate superintendence ; and mainly through his instrumentality and exertions the requisite funds were raised for the completion of the new church at Athens, which was consecrated in the early part of the year 1843 by the Bishop of Gibraltar. Mr. H. D. Leeves was a man of most unaffected and exemplary piety, and in all the relations of life combined in a remarkable degree the meekness and gentleness of the true Christian with great fervency of spirit. His firmness and decision of character, in implicit reliance on his Saviour's purchased gifts, sustained him through many arduous and trying scenes in the difficult position he filled, from which

G

men, equally well-intentioned and of greater physical strength, might almost excusably have shrunk. Every concern of the present life was by him kept in due subordination, and made subservient to the all-important concerns of eternity, and in his presence was always felt that salutary influence which the sincere and consistently practical Christian never fails to impart. His death was the peaceful and happy departure which a life of faith almost invariably ensures. In the spring of the present year, he set out upon a long-projected visit to the Holy Land, and had proceeded as far as Mount Carmel, where an attack of rheumatism and ague obliged him to stay for three weeks in the Latin convent on the Mount. Finding himself become much weaker, he returned to Beirout for the benefit of medical advice, and there closed his earthly career. Until the day before his death, no immediate danger had been apprehended ; but on being then unexpectedly apprised that all hope was over, the intelligence excited no alarm ; he meekly said, ' I could have wished to live a few years longer, not for myself, for I have long served my Saviour, however imperfectly, but for my dear wife and children ; but God's will be done. I am ready to depart, for I know it is far better, though to remain were more needful for them.' An unbroken calm and composure of mind continued to the last ; and one who was a privileged witness of this Christian's death, has stated that those about him could read in the beautiful smile with which he regarded them, how happy the departing spirit was in anticipation of the rest to which it was fleeting."

"J. JAMES."

OBITUARY FROM A GREEK ·PAPER,

No. 46 of the Χρόνος *(" Times"), Athens,* 1845.

"The Rev. Henry Daniel Leeves, priest of the English Church, agent in Greece of the British and Foreign Bible Society, and known for a whole generation to the Greek nation, among whom he had been long settled, departed this life in the Lord, on the 27th of April (old style), at Beirout, in Syria, aged fifty-six, having left the most beloved partner, four daughters, and his first-born son, aged twenty-three.

"When the Rev. H. D. Leeves resided in Constantinople, —where he made the translation of the Holy Scriptures into the vernacular tongue, from the version of the Septuagint, with the consent of the great Church of Christ, through its wise men, Hilarion, Bardalochus, the Holy Sinaite, and others,—the Greek insurrection broke out ; and in those fearful days, when the sword of iniquity was drunk with Christian blood, this celebrated man offered his house as an asylum to many families, and many he saved from the most imminent danger of death. After some time, he removed to Corfu, afterwards to Syra, and lastly to Athens, where he resided for ten years.

" He exhibited so Christian a conversation, that his house, like that of Abraham, was the refuge of the poor and naked. He was in manner cheerful, and easy of address, so that all revered him ; by all was he beloved, by all was he honoured. Always bent on the amelioration and advancement of the nation in which he had resolved to spend the days of his sojourn on earth, he contributed generously, both by word and deed, to the establishment of institutions for the public advantage. There was no charitable society in Greece of which this celebrated man was not a member ; there was no establishment of national benefit for which he was not an active labourer. In particular, having become, in the latter period of his life, the

G 2

proprietor of two estates in Eubœa, he considered it his first duty to form the morals of his villagers (or peasants); and with this view he founded schools, which he maintained at his own expense, supplying them with everything that was necessary, both books and stationery. There is scarcely a district in Greece from which this memorable man has not received letters of thanks for having munificently supplied books to their schools (through the Bible Society). During the whole period of his residence in Greece, he distributed above 100,000 copies of the whole or part of the Holy Scriptures. At last, desiring to salute the holy places where the great mystery of man's salvation was completed, he travelled with one of his daughters, through Smyrna, Rhodes, and Cyprus, to Beirout, where, being attacked by rheumatism and fever, after a month's sojourn, he paid the debt of nature, giving up his perishable body to the earth out of which it had been taken, and his immortal soul into the hands of his Maker, far away from his family, his relatives, and his friends.

"If it be every man's duty to reverence and honour the memory of worthy and virtuous citizens, much more is it the duty of all Greeks to cherish affectionately and perpetually the memory of the Rev. Henry Daniel Leeves. Accept, then, O ever-to-be-remembered man, as a tithe of thy immeasurable goodness to the Greeks, the affection of one Greek, offered to thee with tears, from the depth of the soul of one of thy most beloved friends, for fourteen years conversing with thee, and always admiring thy virtues. Everlasting be thy memory, revered Henry Daniel Leeves! May the Lord give thee rest in the land of the just!"

Trans. by A. M. ELSDALE.

June 1st, 1845.

(Found among Miss LEEVES' MS. papers.)

EXTRACTS FROM A LETTER

From the REV. H. D. LEEVES.

"Athens, June 8th, 1843.

"My dear Niece Anna,

"I know you will be glad to have a line from your old uncle, short soever as it may be, and particularly on his birthday, on which he has completed fifty-four years in this lower world; and although he has had his share, at times, of uneasiness or suffering, yet his judgment is that he is, on the whole, a very happy man, and surrounded with abundant reasons for thankfulness. The present season has been a remarkably successful one, full of prosperity and enjoyment. The main point, the centre of all, has been our own dear little church, which, thank God, was consecrated under the most delightful auspices, and has been since going forward happily and peacefully. It has been, and is, a manifest bond of union, and I promise to ourselves and our community much spiritual good, from bringing out into prominence all the parts of the system of the English Church. I am now, *ipso facto*, Rector of St. Paul's, Athens, though I have no regular appointment from the Government, which, as my friend Henry Addington is Under Secretary of State, and as the situation is, and is likely to be for some time to come, an honorary one, they may perhaps give me; and I like it the better on that account, as long as I have enough without it. This is the first *benefice* I ever had, except my Chaplaincy at Madeira. . . . . Such is the benefit of a Bishop, and of order in a Church. . . . . Our season, however, is nearly over, and in about another fortnight we leave for Castan. . . . . I was at Chalcis last week, and completed the purchase of the Ancient Artemisium for George Wynne. The village is of immense extent, twice, it is said, that of Castan, and has large fine forests, and is very healthy.

. . . . I wish your health were better, and hope the summer will refresh you. . . . . Aunt Bessy appears to be enjoying herself much in her old cot. . . . .

" I enclose you a letter from your Aunt, which will tell you all the news ; so I have nothing more left to say, but to give you my blessing, and sign myself, as ever,

" Your affectionate Uncle,

" H. D. LEEVES."

THE LAST LETTER

Of the Rev. H. D. Leeves *in the " Correspondence of the British and Foreign Bible Society."*

"Athens, February 20, 1845.

" I enclose you herewith a statement of the issues of our Dépôt during the past year. They amount to 8,932 copies, exceeding, by above a thousand, those of last year, although falling short of those of the two or three years preceding. Of these, 7,754 volumes are in the Greek language ; 1,078 in the Greco-Turkish ; and 100 in other languages ; and of the Greek Scriptures, 3,385 volumes are of the New Testament, and 4,369 of the Old Testament, in whole or in part. No journey of distribution has this year been performed, the political circumstances of the country not giving encouragement to it ; but our books have been chiefly sought for in the metropolis, by persons, many of them of consideration, who have desired them for the several provinces to which they belong. By these means they have been sent into the provinces of Attica, Thebes, Acarnania, Doris, Lacedæmon, Maina, Calavrita, Andrizzena, Triphylia, Caritena, Tripolitza, Navarino, Chalcis, and other parts, and have passed through the hands of Governors, Demarchs, Members of the Chamber, Officers, Schoolmasters, and others, and have been devoted to the use of Schools and of private families. Let me extract some few particulars of the mode of their distribution from the notes which now lie before me. To the care of three Schoolmasters in the province of Lacedæmon were intrusted 339 copies; for three Schools in Maina were devoted 175 copies; to the Schoolmaster of Tinos, who was formerly in the service of the Rev. Mr. Hartley during his tour and residence in Greece, 12 Ancient-Greek Testaments for his higher class; to the Demarch of Corinth, a Member of the Chamber of Deputies, were given 228 copies for the Schools of Corinth and the surrounding villages; to the Demarch of Clitoria, in the province of Calavrita, for Schools, 88 copies; to the Demarch of Platæa, for the same purpose, 125 copies; to one of the Members for Corinth, for the Commune of Sicyon, 92 copies; to the Member for Andrizzena, now appointed Governor of a province, for the Schools of Andrizzena and for private distribution, 265 copies; to the Master of the Public School of Selinse, in Calavrita, 140 copies; to that of Selinuntium, in Lacedæmon, 60 copies; to a Deputy for Tryphylia, who has chief influence among the inhabitants of the district of Condovouni, the most warlike of that part of the Peloponnesus, 58 copies; a second donation to the same, 25 copies; to the nephew of a Deputy for Tripolitza, for different friends in that city, 38 copies; to the nephew of a Member of the Senate, the Demarch of an extensive Commune in Acarnania, for the Schools of that district, 438 copies; to the son of a Senator, for his friends in Tripolitza, 25 copies; to a gentleman who has married the daughter of the celebrated Chief Caraiskaki, for distribution among his friends in his native place, a town of Caritena containing 700 families, 86 copies; to the Mistress of the Girls' School at Chalcis 178 copies. This may suffice to show the channels through which our books penetrate and are distributed through various parts of Greece.

The establishment of Mrs. Hill has, as usual, been supplied from our resources, and has received 200 Pentateuchs, 150 Gospels, 250 New Testaments, and 18 Old Testaments, during the year; and I have had the pleasure of sending to Mr.

Hildner, at Syra, for his Schools, which continue steadily to
flourish and to do good, 392 Greek Testaments. He might be
able to furnish us with some interesting details of the advantage
which has· flowed from the continued supplies of the word of
God to his Schools during a series of years; and I have
requested him to send me some statement of the sort, which
when I receive, I will forward to you.

"Occasions also present themselves of sending our Books
advantageously to places in the Turkish dominions, where a
more bitter spirit of opposition prevails than in Greece. To a
Greek of Asia Minor, returning to his native place, I entrusted
30 copies; to a student in the Gymnasium, from Naoussa in
Thessaly, which during the Revolution, was sacked by the Turks,
and numbers of its inhabitants slaughtered or sold into captivity,
I gave 60 copies, to be sent to his friends for distribution ; and
I put into the hands of a Bulgarian physician, who had been
studying in Athens, and was about to return to his country,
95 copies. I should not omit, also, to mention, that our old
Correspondent, the Rev. Mr. Benton, received and put into
circulation, before he finally left the island of Crete and returned
to the United States, the considerable supply of 949 copies."

EXTRACT FROM THE REPORT

Of the British and Foreign Bible Society. 1845.

"Mr. Leeves having offered 4,000 copies of the Modern
Greek New Testament (the printing of which has been completed
at Athens during the year) to the Government, for the use chiefly
of the Public Schools of the kingdom, has been admitted to an
interview with Mr. Coletti, the Prime Minister. He writes :—

"'Upon my stating the matter to him, for which he had been prepared
by the explanations of a common friend, he said he had no doubt that a
translation prepared under the care of Professor Bambas and his coadjutors
was pure in style, and faithful to the original; that the Government would

readily accept the offer I made ; and he only begged me to bring the matter
before him in a regular form, which I have just now done, putting at his
disposition 4000 copies. He fully acknowledged the benefit we are conferring
on Greece; observing that he believed, as a country, she had a great destiny
to fulfil, and that Athens was designed to be again the focus of light and
knowledge to the surrounding nations of the East.

"The revision of the Modern Greek Bible has been
finished by your Agent (Mr. Leeves) and his coadjutors,
principally Professor Bambas, the Rector of the University.
Mr. Leeves has written strongly to urge the printing of an
edition at Athens itself, for which that city affords every facility.
He further advises the addition of the marginal references.
Your Committee have concurred in these views.

"The printing of the Judæo-Spanish New Testament has
been completed at Athens : and the Bishop of Jerusalem has
requested to have 100 copies.

"Mr. Leeves is now on a visit to Palestine."

LETTER TO

THE REV. R. ELSDALE, D.D.

Referring to the REV. H. D. LEEVES, B.D.

"Argos, Feb. 23rd, 1842.

" My dearest Father,

"Your last kind and comforting letter rejoiced me very
much. To be assured of your continual love and prayers, is
always equally sweet and grateful to my heart ; and however
often the tale is told, it seems always new; for we are such
foolish forgetful creatures, that, unless we are continually put in
remembrance, a shade falls over our best joys and feelings.
How one loves to glance back at the sunny spots in one's life,
gladdened by pure affection, which burst out through all the

clouds that obscure this darkened world, no longer living in the light of God's countenance !

" It is only an *idea* that we cannot so well communicate at a distance of thousands of miles ; for there is no distance to the soul. When I think of you, you seem to be as near to me as ever, and I represent everything that has happened in a perfect picture. How happy must the angels be, who can look back upon their whole existence without any self-reproach ; for it is that which often mars the pictures of our memory, and fills the regretful sigh. Yet there is a refuge ;

> ' There is a fountain fill'd with blood,
>   Drawn from Emmanuel's veins ;
> And sinners plunged beneath that flood,
>   Lose all their guilty stains.'

" Oh ! that this were felt by the prisoners whom we saw yesterday in the Palamede of Nauplia, where uncle Henry wished to see again his old aquaintance, Bibisi, formerly a terrible brigand chief. A heavy door was unbarred ; we entered, and were locked in by the gendarme accompanying us. We found ourselves in a large court, open to the sky, with immensely high walls, in which were cells for the prisoners. Here were 15 men, stained with the blood of numbers, confined for life in chains ; seeing only the sky and the dense walls of their prison, the changes of their guards, and the visitors who come with curiosity or compassion to look upon their awful state, or to pour the balm of consolation into their seared hearts. Bibisi came forward, clanking a heavy chain, a square thick-set man of immense strength and lowering brow (the lower part of the face and the neck uncommonly large) ; yet he looked upon my uncle with love (as all do), while he gave him a New Testament, and spoke to him messages from the Gospel of peace. Aunt Bessy sketched him, and gave him the Psalms.

" This was the way in which uncle Henry first saw him. One day, when my uncle and Mr. Acland were descending

Hymettus, three savage-looking men came to them on a crag. After talking a little, my uncle and Mr. Acland thought it best to descend, and were quietly picking their way, when Bibisi called after them, ' We are robbers, but you need not fear, we do not mean to do you any harm ; we never do anybody any harm, we only want bread to eat.' He then enquired ' if there was any likelihood of pardon, if they were to give themselves up, and be willing to change their mode of life.' ' Oh,' said my uncle, ' if that is what you are thinking of, let us sit down and talk about it.' They sat on the crag ; and Bibisi told them how tired he was of his present life, hunted like a wild beast upon the mountains, without bread enough to eat, and that from a soldier he had become a robber. Uncle Henry promised to meet them again the next day, to say what could be done for them. This he did, with Mr. Acland, Mr. Frere, and cousin Henry. The Government did not say that nothing would be done to Bibisi, if he gave himself up ; but promised to deal as favourably with him as they could. To the others they offered pardon ; these have since surrendered. Bibisi is deeply implicated, with the blood of 86 persons upon his hands. He has had many struggles with gendarmes who came to take him ; as he said to my uncle, ' I would give myself up ; but if they come to take me, it will not be without blood.' He was afterwards taken ; and after two attempts to escape, is now consigned for life to the strong fortress of Nauplia.

" We were greatly fatigued in mounting this rocky and rapid ascent. The Polish Commandant and his Smyrniote wife received us most kindly in his melancholy kingdom, refreshed us in his nice house with coffee and music, and then conducted us over the place. First, through the dwellings of the prisoners for a term of years, employed in different trades,—shoemakers, tailors, weavers, &c.,—with German masters, manufacturing raiment for the military. The last we saw, was the enclosure of the prisoners who go no more out ; who have no hope for this world ; and whose sunken eye, and hollow smile, tell of deeds one would not hear.

" The Commandant said he had been there four years ; and that if he were once changed, he would never return. The view from the summit is grand, of the mountains, of Argos and Nauplia, and the rocky coast where Agamemnon was wrecked, when false lights were put out to delude him, on his return from the siege of Troy.

" No more room, my dear father, but to say that I am ever your loving child,

"A. M. E."

LETTER TO MRS. ELSDALE,

On the Death of the REV. H. D. LEEVES.

" Wrington, June 10, 1845.
" My dearest Mother,

*   *   *

" We have the balm of consolation and regret flowing in upon us from every quarter, testifying to the precious jewel of heavenly faith which shone through his earthly life so steadily, and which indeed made him a light to shine in the world. I now feel it a great mercy to have been permitted to dwell so long with him, and to watch his light, so calm and tranquil. I always remarked that his very presence was a check to evil, and a silent influence to good ; and this should be the mark of the Christian, whose eye is turned heavenwards, and no longer wears the impression of the base things of earth. In him I saw exemplified that integrity and reality of character, for which one often sighs in the muddy and troubled waters of this world, where souls are not clear to the touchstone of truth, and where the ' single eye' spoken of by our Saviour is so rare. I remember one day, when we went to the beautiful cemetery at Athens together, he said he thought he should lie there ; but his resting place is at Beirout, on his way to Jerusalem.

*   *   *

" Your affectionate child,

"A. M. E."

EXTRACT OF A LETTER,

From MISS OXENHAM, *on the Death of the* REV. H. D. LEEVES.

"Far be it from us, however, to call in question such a providential dispensation; one, doubtless, sent in love to His faithful servant, who had indeed borne the burden and heat of many a weary day in his Lord's vineyard. Oh! how inexpressibly blessed must the rest of such a labourer be in the peaceful fields of Paradise, beside the still waters of everlasting comfort. How will he, who has been the instrument of turning so many to righteousness, shine like a star in the firmament above!

PART OF A LETTER

From the REV. F. V. J. ARUNDELL, *on the Death of the*
REV. H. D. LEEVES.

" Landulph Rectory, near Devonport,
"July 4th, 1845.

*   *   *

" I have indeed felt, and do feel most deeply, the loss of so dear a friend. Your uncle was so identified with my happiest days at Smyrna, and my days of trial also. I was so sure to find so much kindheartedness, so much consolation, such excellent advice, whenever I applied to him; and he was the only person I was in the habit of corresponding with, when my mind was at all oppressed; so that, though our intercourse, and even correspondence had ceased, or very nearly so, for eight years, the news of his departure from this world of separations, has recalled most vividly every event connected with our former friendship. I can truly say, I never had a friend not immediately connected with my own family, that I loved so much !

"But what a happy death!—how calm, how enviable ! What a privilege, while his heart was set on seeing the earthly city, to have his eyes opened so sweetly on the glories of the holy city above ! Oh ! how I feel for his bereaved widow and family ! Theirs is indeed the suffering, the agony ; his, is all the gain !"

.

LINES

BY

MISS E. LEEVES.

MISS E. LEEVES.

The following lines were found among the papers of Miss E. Leeves, youngest daughter of the Rev. W. Leeves, and are · inserted as forming a connecting link in the family chain.

Miss Leeves has left behind her many evidences of her remarkable musical and artistic gifts, as well as testimonies in the hearts of the poor and afflicted, who were her especial care ; and her life was spent in doing good.

Whilst on a visit to her native village, Wrington, in 1866, she died, after an illness of only two days, " in joy and peace in believing," anticipating the " sacred high eternal noon " to which she was approaching.

Her remains were interred with great respect amidst the resting-places of her revered ancestors ; and her memory is precious to all who knew her.

Death, though sudden, did not find her unprepared ; and how blessed must have been the quick transition to those heavenly joys, of which she had on earth so keen a foretaste ! She once remarked, that " from her earliest childhood, she could not remember a time when she did not love the Lord."

H

SUPPLEMENTAL STANZAS

TO

"SHE WORE A WREATH OF ROSES."

Oh ! once more may I see her
A wreath unfading wear,
Renewed in heavenly beauty,
In robes of white appear,
And standing by her side that one
Whom she on earth loved best,
Free ever in that home of love
From sorrow and unrest.

Oh ! may it be a deathless love ;
For how can mortals bear
To love but for a moment,
And part for ever *there ?*

  *   *   *

Oh ! once again I saw her,
No bridal wreath she wore,—
'Twas cast before the throne of Him
Who all her sorrows bore.
Yes ! once again I saw her
(*Who* would not be above !)
With a voice of endless joy,
In a home of endless love.

She was changed, as in a moment,
In the twinkling of an eye,
To a never-fading creature,
Where no sorrow is, nor sigh.

THE FACTORY.

Written in DR. ELSDALE'S *house opposite the Cathedral, Manchester,*
29th November, 1837.

'Tis early dawn,—'tis ling'ring night,—
And th' church looks dim by th' pale lamp's light.—
Hark ! hark ! what sounds are gath'ring round
Of stirring footsteps' ceaseless sound ;
Resounding all the pavement o'er,
Like distant waters' falling roar ?
In endless flow they stream along,
A mass of life,—but a voiceless throng.
A sounding bell is the voice I hear ;
Does it tell of death to my list'ning ear ?—
It tells, it tells, of the death of life,
Of the weary child, and the pallid wife ;
It tells, it tells, they have left their home, .
And are on their way to their living tomb,—
The wither'd child, and the sickly wife,
And father, subdued with the toils of life,
At the factory door they are pouring in,
To the pond'rous engine's furious din ;
Who, like a greedy monster pent,
Is raging with imprisonment ;
His black breath blotting day's bright beams,
Boiling with passion ; and he seems,
With quiv'ring fury, ceaseless roar,
And thundering beat, to cry, ' more ! more ! '

     *   *   *

'Tis morn again,—and weary feet
Are heard again on the pavèd street ;

H 2

They press to the *Gates*, which open wide,
The child, the man, and the wife at his side.
The bell! the bell! is the voice I hear,
'Tis the voice of mercy,—the gate of prayer!
'Tis the voice of mercy,—they come! they come!
To hear of rest and a heavenly home;
'Tis the footstep of those who keep *holy* day,
When the publican goes to the temple to pray.
They bury their care and their sin together,
All glory to God and the Lamb for ever!
They have leant awhile on Jesu's breast,—
That earthly heaven where the weary rest,—
Confessing to Him with uplifted faces,
" Thou mak'st our lines fall in heavenly places : " *
And they press to the Factory Gate on the morrow,
With more of joy, and less of sorrow.

MY BROTHER GEORGE'S BIRTHDAY.

(He was a Midshipman in the Royal Navy.)

Musings on the 7th of December, 1837.

Thou'rt far away! far, far away!
Oh! would that thou wert near
As thou wert wont in childhood's day,
   My brother ever dear!
We were the youngest of our mother,
Our hearts were closely knit together.
     Our hearts were one,
     But thou art gone,
        My brother!

---

* This was the expression of a young woman who had hurried at the close of her factory, to the weekly meeting of the Bennet Street School. In this establishment there were four stories, each containing a hundred children.

Thine arm around my neck I wore,
  By clasping fingers bound,
As, traversing the garden walks,
  We wander'd all around.
We feasted on the mulberry,
  Beneath the elm we swung,
In our days of youth and infancy,
  Where the golden pippins hung.

We laugh'd at little pussy-cat
  For playing with her tail;
Or scamper'd down with straws to meet
  Old Joseph with the pail.*

We gazed upon the pear-trees' bloom
Which all-enwrapp'd our happy home ;
    And pond'ring on the trees,
    And their orchestra of bees,
We both had nearly tumbled o'er
The spud and weeding-basket's store,
    Our gentle father's† occupation,
    Deep in melodious contemplation ;
His looks were music, and his soul
Under soft harmony's control.

Thus joyously we tripp'd along
To the sweet buzzing bees' bright song;
Our tender mother now appears,
Rejoicing in her " happy dears : "
Her deepest love seem'd fix'd on thee,
But, oh ! not less she lovèd me.

    'Twas then that England's pride,—
    Her life,—her Nelson died !

---

* From milking the cows.
† The composer of " Auld Robin Gray " and much Sacred Music.

We heard the muffled peal of victory and death,
And, listening, held our breath :
Bright deeds and thoughts of glory stole
Into thy steadfast soul.

Thou left us, ere the holy hand
Had pressèd o'er thy brow ;
But the lovely altar of thy birth
Received thy parting vow.

Thy earthly father gave thee
Of thy heavenly Father's bread,
And of the cup to save thee ;
For thee, for *thee* 'twas shed !

From home thou sailèd and its bow'rs,
But we clasp'd thee oft again,
Amid the sweets of garden flow'rs,
Safe from the stormy main.
And we sang thee, " Guide, O guide him
Great Jehovah," o'er the main ;
" May the Great Jehovah hide him ! "
And He sent thee back again.

But now, thou com'st not as before !
Oh ! shall I never see thee more ?

Yes, trust me, we shall meet again,
Though parted long, my dearest brother,
As formerly we met in youth,
Walking in love with one another !

Yes, yes ! my brother, we shall meet
With joy before the judgment-seat ;
For He, whose Word is truth, hath said
Our sins shall not be mentionèd.

MUSINGS AT NIGHT,

From my Window, which looked on the old Collegiate Church and
Churchyard.

'Tis night ;—and I gaze on the holy pile,
I muse in the dubious light awhile,
On the carvèd windows and fret-work fair,
'Mid the fairy touch of the grey mist there,
Where the lengthen'd battlements' fading line
Is faintly lost in the pale moonshine.
Adorn'd with broidery of light
It riseth to my charmèd sight,
Illumined all around ;
And seems " a castle in the air "
Just fall'n unto the ground.
Above, the temple riseth,
Beneath it, lies the tomb ;
Emblems of life and death
In ages still to come.
The pinnacles stand fixèdly
Heaven's finger-posts eternally ;
The finger of the dead below
Doth warn from never dying woe.
From their height and depth the stars are stealing
Their distant points of light revealing ;
And, to my fancy's eye, might be
Pierced through into eternity.
The circling lamps are gleaming,
And the gliding moon is beaming ;
There are lights around, above,—
The dwelling of God's love.

Like jewelry they shine
About the holy shrine,
As brilliants set transparently
'Mid the windows' lovely tracery;
Imaged in ev'ry archèd pane
Heaven is reflected back again.
But I see, I see, as I earnest gaze,
I see in the midst a *ruby's* blaze!
Is it the ruby Mars,
Set round with diamond stars?
It blazeth forth! 'tis red,—
'Tis vanishèd! 'Tis pale—*'tis red!*
Like a bashful maiden crimsonèd.
Is it moonlight sleeping in sweet repose
O'er "the gathered lilies" and blossom'd rose,
Now raised in new beauty, and join'd above
To the bright Rose of Sharon, the rose-tree of love?
Is it the ray of the midnight lamp
Streaming along the churchyard damp,
Throwing a glimmer to light up the dead,
As they lie in their dark and lonely bed?—
Or the stars, as they stud the early grave
Of the loved and lovely,—the fond and brave;
Or looking from out their azure deep,
Through the soft'ning mist as they silent weep
O'er the maiden's tomb, the tomb of her
Who lies in a coffin of blue and silver?*
Or the pale meteor's quiv'ring spark
As it falls on the cold grave, chill and dark;
Trembling through the freezing air
Above the dying in despair;
Shudd'ring through the thick'ning gloom
Hanging around the hopeless tomb,

---

* Miss Patty Wise, a cousin aged eighteen, was buried in Wrington
Church, in a coffin covered with blue cloth, studded with silver stars.

Where lleth in obscurity
The mocker of futurity,
Seal'd in his cold and earthly cell,
The perishing, lost infidel ?
No ! 'tis no cold, reflected light,
It burneth, it burneth by day and by night ;
'Tis the fire in the holy temple burning,
Ere the sacred Day of Rest returning !—
'Tis the warming flame 'midst the holy choir,
Faint emblem of the seraph's fire,
When he chants of the Lamb to his golden lyre
In tones of undulating bliss which never cease,
From rising ecstasy of joy he singing sinks to peace.
Surpassing strains,—by man not understood,—
From fullest joy, to perfect peace in God !

Manchester, 1837.

A SONG OF PEACE.

*   *   *   *

Descending from above,
O'erwhelm our sins with love ;
Thine outspread arms display,
And say, " They're cast away ! "

*   *   *   *

Begin the song, begin
The song that angels sing ;
Begin the song to-day,
To cheer us on our way ;
And e'en again to-morrow,
Between our bursts of sorrow.
We'll sing in time to-day,
In eternity to-morrow.

Athens, 1839.

THE DEAF AND DUMB CHILD'S HYMN.

Jesus, Thou lovest me !
I smile, and think of Thee ;
I smile, and think of Thee,
For Thou hast died for me.

Jesus, to Thee I come,
For I am deaf and dumb :
O speak unto my heart,
And silently impart

The way to go to heaven,
The way to be forgiv'n,
The way from sin to cease,
The way to die in peace.

Then, then my longing ear
Thy trumpet's voice shall hear ;
And then my silent tongue
Shall burst into a song !

For little Emily, Athens, 1840.

THOUGHTS ON MUSIC.

Each heart seeks happiness, for the world is out of tune. Music is a source of pleasure. In infancy our mothers sing to us, and we sink to rest; in childhood we listen to the song of birds and tinkling sheep bells, and are happy ; but in advancing years the music of fountains, birds, and breezes, does not satisfy us, our hearts' depth responds only to tones proceeding from the source of harmony. It was the simple, sacred harp of Jesse's son, which "refreshed" Saul's troubled spirit. How unlike the wild confusion of tumultuous sounds, the music of demons, so frequently imitated !

The true value of things is determined by their duration. Songs of earth end with each fleeting breath ; songs of heaven begin but to be breathed throughout eternity. Heavenly music is the standard of true beauty. We are permitted and invited to join now the angelic choir,—their subjects ours. Let us swell this sublime chorus ; the musicians, all creation ; the object, glory to God and peace on earth ; the subject, creation and redemption. The sweet psalmist of Israel says, " Let us begin the song now, in the house of our pilgrimage ! Let us exalt his name together ! " Let us learn the song which " only the redeemed can learn," inspired by endless discoveries of heights and depths of love and power ! " O come, let us sing unto the Lord ! "—swelling like the voice of many waters, rising like the rush of mighty winds, falling like descending dew, remembering there was " silence in heaven " between the bursts of the ever-new song. Let the " Amens " sweep and sprinkle up into heaven with swelling harmony, then die away, as if you had breathed out your happy soul.

Athens, 9th December, 1840.

THE REUNION.

Discovered floating in the air, in the Cottage Garden, the day after the one passed at Clevedon with old friends. 1844.

How beautiful that day of life
    We journey'd yesterday,
As once again, with early friends,
    We stray'd as formerly !

How beautiful the veil of shade,
    Floating with silent grace
Around the sunny features
    Of nature's lovely face !

How beautiful the holy shrines
That sparkled into light,
Along the distant paths of earth
Unfolded to our sight !

How beautiful the azure sky,
That lured our thoughts above,
To deep and deeper depths of blue,—
The atmosphere of love !

The fragrant firs are swinging
Their incense to the skies ;
The rising lark is singing,
As up towards heaven he flies.

How beautiful to read all day
Sweet nature's book,—all Thine,—
As wand'ring through this day of life,
Waiting for life Divine !

A

BRIEF SKETCH

OF THE LIFE OF

THE REV.

ROBINSON ELSDALE, D.D.

THE REV.

ROBINSON ELSDALE, D.D.

The name of Elsdale originated from Esk-dale, a small property on the banks of the Esk, on the borders of Scotland. One of the family "has seen, in the possession of a lawyer in Spalding, an old title-deed to this property, which dated as far back as the reign of King John."

The following information, dating from the maternal great-grandfather of Dr. Elsdale, and concluding with his brother, was chiefly given by Dr. Elsdale's niece, Miss Anne Field Elsdale, who wrote several interesting works ("Tales of the Martyrs," "Tales for Children," &c.) :—

"The following is extracted from the 'register in the family Bible,' as the most concise and certain information :—

"'GEORGE FIELD, gentleman, of Alderkirk, grandfather of Ann Elsdale (Dr. Elsdale's mother), died 1772, aged 84; he was a pious man.'

"'ANN FIELD, wife of the above George Field, died 1779, aged 84, full of days and good works.'

"'SUSANNA GIBBINS, daughter of George and Ann Field, mother of Ann Elsdale, died August 29, 1768, aged 30, leaving five children to bewail their great loss.'

"'ANN GIBBINS, daughter of James and Susanna Gibbins, was born November 28th, 1758 or 59, in Spalding.'

"The above extracts in the family Bible are in the writing

of Ann Elsdale (the mother of Dr. Elsdale) ; the following entry
is in that of Robinson Elsdale (the father of Dr. E.) :—

"'ROBINSON ELSDALE and ANN GIBBINS were married, March 31,
1779, at Surfleet Church.'
"'ROBINSON, son of Robinson and Ann Elsdale, was born on Wednesday, March 26, 1783, at Surfleet.'

"'ROBINSON ELSDALE died October 15, 1783, aged 39.'
"'ANN, widow of Robinson Elsdale, died at Surfleet, December 6th,
1837.'

The following relates to the great-grandfather, father,
mother, and brother of Dr. Elsdale :—

"George Field, gentleman, of Alderkirk, as he is described
in the family Bible, the maternal great-grandfather of Dr. Elsdale,
who died in 1772, was also fond of literature ; a large folio
volume of his poems, with which he beguiled the sufferings of
a long affliction, remain as a memorial. His granddaughter, the
mother of Dr. Elsdale, from whom I learnt the few particulars
I know of those who had gone before, and who had been
brought up by him, used to speak of him as so good and
resigned ; while her favourite expression with regard to her
grandmother (his wife) was, that she was ' piety personified.'

"Robinson Elsdale, father of Dr. Elsdale, entered as a
midshipman in the royal navy; but left it, and was afterwards
captain of a merchant vessel. He married on his return from
his last voyage, and had two sons. His widow always spoke of
him as a man of strong sense ; and he left a proof of his literary
taste, in a volume of the adventures of his seafaring life.

" He resided at Surfleet, on the estate which had been in
the family for many generations, and died there, October 15th,
1783, when his youngest son Robinson (Dr. E.) was little more
than six months old. His mother's maiden name was Robinson.
His wife (whose maiden name was Gibbins) was brought up by
her grandparents, Mr. and Mrs. Field. Her grandmother, it
appears, died in the same year that she was married. I think
her father lived at Surfleet then (and I believe in the house at
the Bridge), which would account for her being married there.

" Mr. Elsdale lived in a house about a mile from the Church, in which his wife passed the few years of her married life, and fifty-four of widowhood. She was a very sensible woman, and must have trained her two sons most judiciously, if we may judge from the after lives of both. I believe both were considerably above the average standard of learning and intellectual attainments of their day; and both shewed plainly that they sought a better country. They were both strikingly indifferent to many things which most people think so much of; and they had peculiar ways of interweaving religious thoughts into every-day life.

" The elder son, the Rev. Samuel Elsdale, took his degrees of ' B.A., February 17, 1803, and of M.A., June 21, 1809.' He was ' a most excellent man, highly intellectual, and deeply religious. He was a frequent writer in the ,' Gentleman's Magazine ; ' and amongst other literary productions, left a volume of sacred poetry. He was for some years Headmaster of the Grammar School at Moulton, where he died, and was buried, at the age of 47."

The younger son, Robinson, the subject of the following memoir, was born March 26th, 1783. He was at School at Uppingham, and was admitted to a scholarship at Corpus Christi College, October 16th, 1801 (" Scholar in right as Fellow," as it then was). At that time he used to study sixteen hours a-day. The dates of his degrees are as follows, extracted from the " Catalogue of Oxford Graduates, 1851," just republished :— " Robinson Elsdale, C.C.C., B.A., June 12th, 1805 ; M.A., Feb. 1, 1807; B. and D.D., July 7, 1838." In 1808, he was appointed to the Second Mastership of the Manchester (then) Free Grammar School. On the 28th of May, 1809, he received Deacon's Orders from " Charles, Bishop of Oxford ; " on the 24th of December, 1809, he received Priest's Orders from the same. On the 24th of July, 1810, he vacated his scholarship

I

by marriage, at Wrington, with Marianne, eldest daughter of the Rev. William Leeves, Rector of Wrington, Somerset.

Mr. Leeves' father, in the parchment from the Herald's Office, granting the "arms and crest assigned to him, August 1st, 1741," is thus described,— "Henry Leeves, of Kensington, in the county of Middlesex, Esqr., son of John Leeves, of the same county."

Mr. Leeves' maternal grandparents were Mr. and Mrs. Buller. Their daughter, Miss Buller, married Henry Leeves, Esq., father of the Rev. W. Leeves.

Dr. Elsdale was appointed "Domestic Chaplain to Anne, Dowager Countess of Manvers, October 26th, 1818, in the fifty-ninth year of the reign of George III."

Dr. Elsdale had Curacies at Cheetham Hill and Chorlton, and was appointed Incumbent of Stretford in 1819. He was devoted to his duties, giving at least one half-holiday, besides the Sundays, to parochial work. He annually visited his revered mother at Surfleet till her death, December 6th, 1837.

"In 1837 he was appointed Highmaster of the Manchester Grammar School.

Love and charity to all formed his general characteristics.

His last days of peace and patient suffering, alleviated and soothed by the kindness of all his friends, were spent at Wrington; from whence he passed tranquilly to "the rest that remaineth for the people of God," leaving his family to lament their irreparable loss, while they rejoiced in his eternal gain. He had thirteen children, seven of whom survive. Others have kindly traced the character he sustained as a true and humble Christian, advancing in likeness to his Saviour as he neared the goal of his wishes,—the time when he would be "for ever with the Lord."

His epitaph, written by himself, and afterwards placed on his tombstone at Wrington, is as follows :—

"ROBINSON ELSDALE, D.D.

"Born March 26th, 1783.   Died August 8th, 1850.*

"'What must I do to be saved?'
"'Believe on the Lord Jesus Christ, and thou shalt be saved.'
"'Faith without works is dead.'
"'God is love.'"

---

* Added afterwards.

OBITUARY NOTICES.

From the MANCHESTER COURIER, *August,* 1850.

"DEATH OF DR. ELSDALE.—Our obituary of to-day records the death, at the ripe age of sixty-seven, of the Rev. Dr.
Robinson Elsdale, formerly highmaster of the Manchester Free
Grammar School. The Rev. Dr. died at Wrington, near Bristol.
He was a native of Lincolnshire, and was elected to a scholarship
in Corpus Christi College, Oxford, on the foundation of a school
in his native county, where he was educated. In 1808, when he
had taken his degree of B.A., he was appointed by the president
of his College to the second mastership, and was remarkable,
nay proverbial, for the punctuality with which he attended upon
his duties. To the extent of his acquirements and his capa-
bilities as a tutor, the solid attainments of many of his pupils
now living testify. He was an excellent master, and as a man,
highly respected and beloved."

From the MANCHESTER COURIER, *August 30th,* 1850.

"On Thursday, the 8th inst., at Wrington, near Bristol,
aged sixty-seven years, deeply-lamented by his family and
friends, the Reverend Robinson Elsdale, D.D., Incumbent of
Stretford, formerly second, and subsequently high master of the
Free Grammar School in this town ; the duties of which offices
he discharged with the greatest fidelity for nearly thirty years.
He lived the life of a true Christian, and his end was peace."

INSCRIPTION ON A TABLET

Placed in Moulton Church.

SACRED

TO THE MEMORY OF

THE REV. SAMUEL ELSDALE, M.A.,

LATE FELLOW OF LINCOLN COLLEGE, OXFORD,

AND MASTER OF THE FREE GRAMMAR SCHOOL IN THIS PLACE.

HE DIED 13TH JULY, 1827,

AGED 47 YEARS.

Give alms of thy goods, and
Never turn thy face away
From any poor man, and
Then the face of the Lord
Shall never be turned
Away from thee.
Tobit, chap. 8, verse 7.

EXTRACT FROM A SERMON

On the Death of the REV. ROBINSON ELSDALE, D.D., *by the*
REV. HENRY THOMPSON, M.A. *Vicar of Chard.*

(Sermon on St. Luke xx. 38, preached in Wrington Church,
August, 1838.)

"If we sorrow over those who depart in the fulness of
years, we yet rejoice that they have long glorified God, laid up
abundant treasure in heaven, cast off pains and infirmities for
ever, put on strength and knowledge, been gathered into the
eternal garner 'as a shock of corn cometh in his season.' Such
a loss have we now to lament; the meek disciple and faithful
steward: faithful in all his house,—pattern and preceptor of his
children,—sufferer himself with Christ, and glorifying Him by
Christian patience,—whose favourite text was, 'God is love;'
who kept that truth before his heart no less than before his eyes,
having it inscribed in his chamber, that he might always look
upon it, as it was inscribed on his last house, that it might meet
his first glance in the resurrection; who dwelt in love, and
therefore, we humbly believe, was partaker of the blessing, 'he
that dwelleth in love dwelleth in God, and God in him;' who
ever felt assured that 'all was for the best'; who was resigned to
live (for with him life, rather than death, needed resignation),
but was ever ready to die: suffering ofttimes so much as to feel
the chastisement hard to bear,—to feel that life would not be
worth having, but for the happy sleep and glorious waking to
follow,—that the negative happiness of heaven, the mere
exemption from pain, was no less than positive bliss,—trying
to support his sufferings (these were his very words) 'by the
hope of the painless, complete, eternal happiness of heaven,
through Christ.' Looking at the sufferings of Christ, and

praying and trying to be more patient through Him, and succeeding too, through Christ that strengthened him ; forward, while a remnant of strength subsisted, to visit the sick and afflicted,—the advocate and example of peace, love, and good-will to all. In this visitation we all seek comfort, and some deeply need it. But our consolation aboundeth by Christ, and in the words of the text we shall find it treasured for us abundantly."

TO THE MEMORY

OF THE

REV. ROBINSON ELSDALE, D.D.,

Highmaster of the Free Grammar School, Manchester,
and Incumbent of Stretford.

———

'Tis night ;—and in the deep blue vault of heaven
Innumerable stars are shining forth
In tranquil beauty o'er the silent earth ;—
The noise and tumult of the day are past,
And all around breathes peace and holy calm.

In dream-like reverie I sit and muse,
Till fancy calls up visions of old times.
My thoughts fly back e'en to the summer hours
When in fair Kersal's Woods I loved to roam
With blithesome friends in sweet companionship ;
To happy school-days, when the dull routine,
The irksome task of learning, was made light
By Elsdale's genial wisdom ; bringing out
From his rich storehouse illustrations apt
Of modern thought and study, that oft flashed
A meaning new upon the mystic page
Of ancient oracles, drawing out the soul
And spirit of the past.   Beneath his spell

The forms of old philosophy were girt
With fresher beauty, glowed with nobler life!

Oh! happy days! how quickly ye flew by!—
And thou, loved Tutor! how thy memory lives
In grateful hearts of those (alas! how few!)
Who yet survive to bless thy loving care
And precepts of deep wisdom; sounding quaint
To buoyant youth, but in the after years
How well-remembered, when, amid life's cares,
Thy deep-toned voice seemed ringing once again
With words of power to animate the soul,
And rouse it from despair and listlessness;
Bidding it shun the heights precipitous,
Where bold ambition lures to Fame and—Death!
To love the simple vale where Duty lies;
To turn aside from speculation rash,
And all that cannot bear the searching light
Of God's pure law; to spurn the shifty rule
(That deems success the synonym of right)
Of low expediency, and to found
Each action on the eternal rock of Truth;
To scorn the sordid trickeries of the world,
And all the little meannesses of trade!

My soul doth thank thee for thy lessons sage,
Which have to me a beacon been, and star,
Amid the dark intricacies of life
And questionable morals of the age!

Oh! saintly-hearted Elsdale! thou didst bend
And sacrifice at holy Duty's shrine
The highest powers of intellect; content
To live unnoticed, and to die unknown
(At least to mortal fame), so thou might'st win
Thy erring brethren to the love of Christ,
Whose banner 'twas thy privilege to bear
With faith unfaltering!

May thy sons accept
This feeble tribute to their father's worth
From one who loved him living, mourned him dead ;
Thankful for all his lessons of high Truth
And bright example !

C. G. R.

Oct. 15, 1871.

THE MANCHESTER GRAMMAR SCHOOL.

" There were Giants " even " in those *days."*

" Vixere fortes ante Agamemnona."

"TO THE EDITOR OF THE 'MANCHESTER COURIER.'

" Sir,

" The recent proceedings and speeches at the Dinner of the Trustees of the Manchester (alas ! no longer Free) Grammar School, when Lord Derby presided, have led me to think of old times, when I had the pleasure of sitting at the feet of Dr. Elsdale as my Gamaliel. It struck me that the teaching of the old system produced as fine a fruit as the new promises to do ; that sound truths were instilled into us, drawn from Holy Scripture,—not flimsy theories of fanciful philosophy ; and that it would be well to remind the present generation of the merits of past masters, who have been rather disparaged by the almost fulsome laudation of the present system, masters, trustees, and all.

"AN OLD SCHOLAR.

" 31*st Oct.*, 1871."

(CHARLES GEORGE RHODES.)

A LETTER

From the same.

" Dear Madam,

"I do not think I can add much to the sketch I have already given of your beloved father's character ; but I may just add, that his simplicity and earnestness always seemed to me remarkable, as also his love for children, and his devotion to the duties of his position. Nothing but love and duty could have sustained him so long in the drudgery of teaching the lower forms. His conscientiousness won him the respect and veneration of his pupils. It was his delight to do whatever he had to do, *well;* and his boys always went forward well-grounded in grammar and those primary studies which form the basis of all sound classical learning. His aim, however, was to make his pupils not only ripe classical scholars, but Christian scholars also. He had a bright intellect, which was competent to hold its own in all branches of study; and his rich illustrations, drawn from varied sources, imparted a charm to his teaching, which, in modern times, may be equalled, but cannot be surpassed. I remember, when the daily tasks were finished, before the time for prayers, how he would call us up to read an extra chapter of Greek or Roman history, or what he loved better, a chapter from the Bible ; not making it task-work, but rather a privilege and reward for our conduct during the day.

" Chief above all,
He held the Word of God in reverent love ;
And ever and anon, from sacred tome,
Would choose the themes that to his thirsty soul
Had borne, in flood of holiest delight,
Rich draughts of joy and sweet deliciousness ;
In hope that we, won by Christ's tenderness,
And drawn unto Him as by cords of love,

Might quaff, from the same fount of heavenly peace,
The streams of living water that made glad
The Paradise of God ; and by His Spirit led,
Might win like blessing, strength to do His Will,
And, with unspotted robes, to walk unscathed
Amid the wild temptations of the world,
And Satan's subtle snares ; our hope His cross,
Who ' died that we might live ' and ever reign
With Him in glory in the life to come !

"One interesting fact I must not omit to mention. At the time when the cholera visited Manchester, about 1832, the Grammar School was closed, and the pupils dispersed to their respective homes. Dr. Elsdale, during this period, gathered together such of his pupils as he could, at his house in Strangeways, and attended to their instruction as carefully as if the School had been open. I was not, at that time, under his care at the School, but I was one of those privileged to attend at his house ; and I shall never forget his kindness. All this was done without hope of fee or reward.

"I remember your father once saying, 'Boys, I hope neither you nor I may ever come suddenly to any great fortune or honour. I am sure it would turn my brain, and I fear it would yours also.'

"If I have succeeded, in any way, in reviving the memory of your saintly father, I have to some small extent realized my wish of doing honour and showing my gratitude to him,—a wish I have never been able to accomplish until now.

"Perhaps some of his other old pupils will be able to fill up the details of this imperfect sketch.

"With deep respect for your father's memory,

"I remain, Madam,
"Yours faithfully,
"CHAS. GEO. RHODES.
"To Mrs. Moon."

LETTERS

From the same, conveying Extracts from Letters to him from former Pupils and Friends of DR. ELSDALE'S.

"December 16th, 1871.

"Dear Madam,

*   *   *

"The following extract from the letter of a clerical friend, will, I am sure, gratify you :—

'The excellent Preceptor whose memory your piety has 'embalmed, after so graceful a manner, I used to hear of in my 'younger days, from boys who had been at the Grammar School, 'and their testimony was always of a favourable kind. Amiable 'and much-beloved, he seemed to be ; moreover, I always 'considered him one of whom the world was not worthy. 'Doubtless he awaits, and will receive, a much higher reward 'than any *it* has the power to bestow.' "

"*From* CHARLES MEREDITH, ESQ. *(Manchester.)*

"December 22nd, 1871.

'I have a very grateful recollection of Dr. Elsdale ; he 'behaved most kindly to me, and in one instance advanced me 'and Mark Ringham, a fellow scholar, six months before the 'usual time, from a Latin to a Greek class, and gave us instruction 'in Greek thrice a-week, at his residence, during the Christmas 'holidays, to prepare us for the advancement on the re-opening 'of the school ; for which he would receive no remuneration.'

*   *   *

"I am told that your father's old parishioners, at Stretford, still retain a grateful remembrance of his labours.

*   *   *

" I heartily thank you and Dr. Moon for your good wishes, and sincerely and warmly reciprocate them.

" With sincere respect and kind regards,
" Believe me,
" Ever yours faithfully,
"CHAS. GEO. RHODES."

LETTER AND SKETCH

By the Rev. J. C. Bagshaw, M.A. *(Domestic Chaplain to the Right Hon. Viscount Hill).*

" Chaplain's House, Hawkstone,
" March 1st, 1872.
" Dear Mrs. Moon,

*　　　　*　　　　*

" I am very thankful to have the opportunity of adding my tribute to your dear father's worth.

*　　　　*　　　　*

" It is so long since I left Manchester School, that many early associations have, as a matter of course, become weakened and indistinct. Nothing, however, clings so to one's memory as old school days; and none of those who were under Dr. Elsdale, at the time of which I am writing,—when he was Second Master,—can ever forget him, or his patient instruction and faithful admonitions.

" As a Master, he was particularly remarkable for a *patient discharge of duty*, and a *strict sense of justice.*

" He was always at his post, always *punctual*, thus enforcing punctuality on his pupils by his own example. A strict disciplinarian—(too strict no doubt some of us thought),—he could yet unbend. No one enjoyed a merry laugh more than himself; and no one delighted more to give pleasure. After a 'long grammar lesson' (one of the 'institutions' of his classes), when pleased with his boys, he would give all the class a treat.

So, with individual boys, he was always glad to show how much he was pleased with them. It is one of my pleasant recollections of school days, that I often received from him some little reward, when he had been pleased with the day's work.

"But his strict *justice* and *impartiality* were always most religiously maintained. I do not think it could fairly be said that he showed favour towards any one of his pupils. I was sometimes tempted to think that he was most strict towards those to whom he seemed most drawn. In the school, he dealt with all alike. His integrity as a master was unquestionable.

. "Living out of town, it was my lot to be, for a time, under his Ministry. He was then Incumbent of Stretford. I can well call to mind his appearance in the Desk and Pulpit, and his earnest loving appeals to his Congregation.

"As a Pastor, *humility* was a striking feature in his character; and this humility deepened, as was to be expected, as years rolled on. His memory is still affectionately cherished by many of his former parishioners.

*　　　*　　　*

"He was always thoughtful about the people among whom he had so long ministered. The letters which I had the happiness to receive from him when at College, and afterwards when in Orders, always showed how constantly he prayed for his old charge; many of his people were specially mentioned in his prayers.

"His *simplicity* of character was very marked. His firm trust in the merits and work of the Lord Jesus Christ could not be hidden. He shrank from a display of his Christian life; but it was seen, and noted. He was not perfect, he had his peculiarities; yet it would be well for us if simplicity and purity of character, humility and self-denial, a spirit of prayer, and firm trust in our blessed Lord, such as were found in Robinson Elsdale, were found in all Christians.

"His memory and his example are an encouragement and a comfort to me, as, I doubt not, to others of his pupils who survive."

EXTRACT FROM AN

"ODE TO THE MANCHESTER FREE GRAMMAR SCHOOL."

By HENRY WHEELER, *a former Pupil of* DR. ELSDALE'S *(written at the age of Sixteen).*

" I deem thee, viewing thus thy form,
An eagle mounting o'er the storm ;
For thou,—amidst a troubled world,
By wars oppress'd, by tempests hurl'd,—
Thou, thou, whilst many a mortal name
Has perished, standest thus the same.

* * *

" Some forms are graven on the heart
That never, save with life, can part ;
And thou, whilst memory yet may stay
To guide one thought of nature's clay,
Shalt live, by me forgotten not,
When time shall other visions blot.

" Still, whilst I bend at mortal shrine,
And say this day on earth is mine,
My conscious heart, in secret glee,
Shall vibrate as I think on thee ;
Whilst I, through life's declining days,
Will tell thy virtues, sing thy praise.

" O may'st thou stand thus proud and high,
When humbler works of man shall die ;
May'st thou o'er others' pathway shine
A beacon, bright as shone o'er mine ;
And form, through many a coming age,
The fairest gem in history's page."

ON THE MANCHESTER FREE GRAMMAR SCHOOL.

By LAMAN BLANCHARD, 1842.

"In the Manchester Free Grammar School, which was founded early in the sixteenth century, many persons, eminent for science and learning, have been educated. The list extends as far back as the reign of Mary, opening with the well-known name of John Bradford, who suffered martyrdom in 1555; Reginald Heber (the father of the Bishop) was here; Cyril Jackson, and his brother, the Bishop of Oxford; the first Lord Alvanley; Mr. Morritt, of Rokeby; David Latouche, the celebrated banker; the present Mr. Justice Williams, W. Harrison Ainsworth, and many others."

From W. HARRISON AINSWORTH, ESQ.
"Little Rockley, Hurstpierpoint,
"Dec. 23rd, 1871.
"My dear Madam,
*   *   *

"I had not seen Mr. Rhodes' tribute to your excellent father's memory. I have read the lines with much interest, and share the sentiments they express. For Dr. Elsdale I had the warmest attachment. He was a good man, a good Christian, a good divine, and a sound scholar. He was as strict a disciplinarian as his predecessor, Mr. Lawson; and he was as much beloved as Lawson by his pupils.

*   *   *

"Sincerely reciprocating your good wishes,
"Believe me, my dear Madam,
"Very truly yours,
"W. HARRISON AINSWORTH.
"To Mrs. Moon."

From W. HARRISON AINSWORTH, ESQ.

"Little Rockley, Hurstpierpoint,
"March 21st, 1872.
"My dear Mrs. Moon,

*　　*　　*

"One little incident I will mention while it occurs to me. One day, when I was about 16, I was walking with James Montgomery, the poet. We were crossing the churchyard of the present Cathedral, when we encountered your father, who stopped me to make some observations,— not perhaps very flattering,—on a poetical effusion which I had sent him. Montgomery stood by, and heard what was said ; and as we moved on, he remarked, with a good-humoured laugh, 'You have a severe critic there.' I explained that the critic was my tutor, and was entitled to speak plainly to me. Afterwards, when I told Dr. Elsdale that my companion was no other than Montgomery, he was quite vexed that I had not introduced him. (This circumstance is mentioned in Montgomery's Biography.) I shall never forget his look of surprise when I told him Montgomery (for whom he had a great admiration) had been with me. 'WHY DIDN'T you introduce him to me ?' he exclaimed.

*　　*　　*

"I wish I had a better memory and more leisure.
"Pray make my best remembrances to your mother,

"And believe me,
"Very sincerely yours,
"W. HARRISON AINSWORTH."

From C. H. Rickards, Esq.

"Manchester.

April 3rd, 1872.

"Dear Sir,

*   *   *

"I have a most sincere respect for the memory of the late Dr. Elsdale, as a man who most conscientiously did his duty.

"You will probably remember that he at one time held the then incumbency of Stretford ; and I have a distinct recollection of seeing several of his pupils frequently walk on Sundays to service at Stretford, taking their dinners with them. This, even, as a lad, impressed me with the conviction that this could only be the result of appreciative conviction of high principle.

"Fifty years ago, there was not much done by the general body of the clergy in the way of pastoral visitation. There was a scholar of the name of Jackson, who lived in Hulme, and who died. Dr. Elsdale visited the poor fellow, and prayed with him, which told greatly on the whole school.

Dr. E. had a great dread of his pupils catching cold from wet clothes : this care and good-nature occasionally got imposed upon by would-be truants.

*   *   *

"I remain, dear Sir,

"Yours truly,

"C. H. RICKARDS.

"C. G. Rhodes, Esq."

From I. S. PIXTON, ESQ., *to* C. G. RHODES, ESQ.

"Thorn Villa, Urmston,
"Near Manchester.
"Dear Sir,
"Dr. Elsdale was a very great favourite with my late mother, who used to render him much assistance in Church matters.

* * *

"During the early part of the Doctor's incumbency at Stretford, the population was very small; the lower classes, for want of education, very rough and ignorant, especially in spiritual matters. At that time it was not deemed necessary to give the humbler classes any but a very inferior education, such as was given to Mrs. Hind's charity children,—known as the 'green scholars,' all being dressed in green clothes. Hence the great difficulty the Incumbent experienced in imparting to them spiritual instruction, besides his time being very limited, owing to his residing in Manchester.

"In those days there were no conveyances between Stretford and Manchester. The Doctor had therefore to walk both ways, also visiting the sick, as well as on Wednesday afternoon, generally calling on my mother for information on this and any other matters connected with the Church; my mother very frequently in his absence, and with his concurrence, reading to the sick. The Doctor was always very regular in his attendance, and was held in high estimation by his parishioners.

* * *

"I remain,
"Yours very truly,
"I. S. PIXTON."

"When MR. KELLY was Churchwarden in 1864, at the time the REV. T. D. COX MORSE was Rector, he had a Stone Tablet put up in Stretford Church, in commemoration of its rebuilding, containing the following inscription" :—

THE PAROCHIAL CHAPEL,

BUILT A.D. 1718 ON THE SITE OF A FORMER VERY ANCIENT CHAPEL, BEING TOO SMALL FOR THE INCREASED POPULATION OF THE PARISH,

THIS CHURCH WAS ERECTED A.D. 1842.

ROBINSON ELSDALE, D.D., *Incumbent.*

JOSEPH CLARKE, M.A., *Curate in sole Charge.*

GEORGE BANNISTER
WILLIAM BRUNDRIT } *Churchwardens.*

Information received from MR. KELLY, 1872.

"Formerly all the Churches in the parish of Manchester, with the exception of S. John's, S. Mary's, and S. Ann's, were merely Chapels of Ease to the Collegiate Church (now the Cathedral); but by the Manchester Rectory Division Act, a separate district (called a parish) was assigned to each Church, and its Incumbent became a Rector.

"Under this Act of Parliament, Stretford became a Rectory in 1854. Prior to that date, the Minister was styled 'Incumbent.'

"The old Parochial Chapel of Stretford was rebuilt in 1718, and enlarged in 1821 and 1824, and contained about 450 sittings. It was taken down in 1844.

"The new Parochial Church was commenced re-building Sept. 30. 1841; consecrated Oct. 10, 1842; and contains 917 sittings.

"The old Chapel Yard is occasionally used for interments.

J 2

It is well kept; and the Trees planted by Dr. Elsdale are a great ornament.

"There are 7 ancient Chapelries in the parish of Manchester, —viz., Stretford, Chorlton, Didsbury, Gorton, Denton, Newton, and Blackley. The histories of Chorlton, Didsbury, Denton, and Blackley, have been written by the Rev. John Booker, a son-in-law of the late Bishop of Manchester (Dr. Lee.)"

"THE CHRISTIAN WARFARE."

The following Poem is added here, as "it was a favourite of DR. ELSDALE's, and was in many respects a portraiture of his own life and character." It is from the pen of the REV. HENRY THOMPSON, M.A., Vicar of Chard, and appeared in the "*Iris*" for 1830.

"Take up the Cross, and follow Me!"—
  Heard ye the call divine?
Soldier! brace on thy panoply!
  Advance thy Captain's sign!
Conqu'ring, to conquer forth He goes;
By thy weak arm His might can crush His proudest foes.

With Truth's unsullied baldrick gird
  Upon thy mailèd side
The Spirit's glaive, thy Leader's Word;
  Let Virtue's corslet, tried
In strife and furnace, guard thy breast,
And let Salvation's helm thy dauntless brows invest.

But most, upon thy martial arm
  Take Faith's impervious targe,
To quench the fiery shafts of harm,
  Amid the deadly charge.
Then forth on thy victorious way
Speed on, thy steps prepared on Love reveal'd to stay.

Saw'st thou the waters foaming high ?—
    'Tis Passion's restless sea :
Heard'st thou the storm that swept the sky ?—
    'Tis stern Adversity.
Heed not—tread on—the billows, cleft,
Shall fence with crystal wall thy right-hand and thy left.

Saw'st thou the broad and arid plain ?—
    No shelt'ring leaf is there ;
No fount, where scorch'd and fainting pain
    Beneath the sultry glare
May slake his lips.—Nor fear, nor fly :
Heaven's stores shall ope for thee when earth and wave deny.

Greater and mighter far than thou
    The hosts that bar thy way :
Yet let not that high spirit bow :
    A loftier Power than they
Conducts thy march. Before Him driven,
Melts Anak's Titan horde, and rampire wall'd to heaven.

True, dark Ingratitude is there,
    And Disappointment cold ;
And mean Suspicion, from his lair,
    Unwinds his viper fold.
Yet fear not: He, whose knight thou art,
With energy divine can nerve thy human heart.

True, Earth, in treacherous charms array'd,
    With eye too wildly sweet,
Would seek to her unhallow'd shade
    To lure thy pilgrim feet.
Yet yield not : She who woos thy vows
With crown of bleeding thorn enwreath'd thy Master's brows.

Say not, thy yoke is hard to bear;
But think of Him who bore,
For thee, a weightier load of care,
And then repine no more.
His yoke is light, His ways are rest;
They that endure with Him, with him, too, shall be blest.

Fear not, and thou shalt overcome;
Yea, through His love who led,
With palm of more than conquest's bloom
Twine thine unhelmèd head.
'Mid white-robed hosts of fair renown,
The Morning-Star shall shine first jewel of thy crown.

Fear not! in victory thou shalt stand
Upon the glassy sea,
And chant, with heaven's own lyre in hand,
The pæan of the free:
" Sing to the Lord!" the fight is done!
The fearful foe is whelm'd! the rest eternal won!

THE

LAST DAYS

OF

MRS. ELSDALE.

WARMINGTON CHURCH

WARWICKSHIRE

THE LAST DAYS

OF

MRS. ELSDALE,

Widow of the REV. ROBINSON ELSDALE, D.D., *formerly Incumbent of Stretford, and Highmaster of the Manchester Free Grammar School.*

Since the foregoing pages were written, my beloved mother (Mrs. Elsdale), in her 84th year, has passed away to the "rest that remaineth for the people of God."

The addition of a brief memorial of her has been thought desirable, and a requisite sequel to the former reminiscences of the Leeves family.

For about eight years and a-half she had suffered from various physical afflictions; but, amidst them all, her praises and thanksgivings were constantly raised to her Heavenly Father, for all his great mercies and benefits towards her.

During about seven years (since my marriage), her almost daily correspondence with me was but little interrupted, except from incapacity caused by attacks of illness, and the occasions of my annual visits to her.

My last visit commenced on the 11th of June, 1874, and was continued during seven weeks, till the day of her death.

Although for several years she had been suffering from

paralysis of the left side, her mind was calm and her "intellect clear" to the last. In consequence of her helplessness, she had to be wheeled in her chair to the head of the table in the dining-room, where she would often remain after breakfast, occupying her time in reading, writing, and conversing. Until the day of her death, she was generally present both at the morning and evening family prayers at half-past eight.

It was wonderful and very touching, to see the patience and cheerfulness with which she bore her various infirmities, feeling that "underneath" her were "the Everlasting Arms." She once remarked, "The Lord has dealt very wisely with me."

In writing to me a week before my last visit, she said, "In faith and hope I now wait, and watch, and pray for the sweet joy and delight of the heavenly state. I am, I trust, ripening for heaven."

She would sometimes "talk of heaven so earnestly," as to weep with joy at the thought of meeting all her beloved ones there, and of dwelling in the presence of her Lord for ever; and to exclaim, "I want to go to heaven! Oh! glorious place!—such as no one can ever conceive of!"

Music delighted and soothed her; and when seemingly unable to bear with other things, she would, with great pleasure, sit and listen to it for a long time, and occasionally attempt to join in singing, as though anticipating the praises of God in heaven. She was frequently reading the New Testament, a favourite book of Prayers, the "Mountains of Bread" series, and other sweet little books, which staid and refreshed her wearied spirit while lingering on the confines of mortality, and stretching its pinions ready to depart from its failing earthly tabernacle. Once, when reading to her the 77th Psalm, and arriving at the 8th verse, "Is His mercy clean gone for ever, and is His promise come utterly to an end for evermore?" she exclaimed with much fervour, "No it isn't; I *know* it isn't!"

Daily, with her unparalyzed right hand (having a weight on the paper to steady it) she wrote to one or more of her "dear children," or friends.

When I took my leave of her to return to Brighton, on the morning of the 29th of July, she gave me one of her frequent, fervent, and touching blessings; and from her earnest desire to see the last of me in my departure, she accompanied me with her devoted attendant, in the carriage to the station. She seemed to enjoy the drive, and talked of coming to Brighton again " someday." On returning, she called at a friend's house, and spoke of late occurrences. On arriving at home again, after dining, she wrote a letter to one of my brothers, and afterwards commenced one to me. She seemed very restless towards the evening. One of her kind attendants finished reading to her " Naomi and Ruth " (in " Mountains of Bread " series), which she enjoyed; and on hearing the lines,

> " I shall wear a glittering crown on my brow ;
> If ever I loved thee, my Jesus, 'tis now,"

she desired them to be read a second time. She afterwards supped in the balcony, enjoying the sweet refreshing air, which was always grateful to her. At about 10 o'clock she was attacked with another stroke of paralysis, and after an interval of five minutes, without a sigh or struggle, she passed away,

> " Safe in the arms of Jesus ! "

" Her departure was most peaceful ; and she looked indeed (after death) more sweetly asleep than she had done for a long time, and her calm face resumed much of its former aspect."

> " They die in Jesus, and are bless'd ;
> How kind their slumbers are !
> From sufferings and from sins released,
> And freed from every snare."

Such was her delightful release from a world of sin ! So sudden, so peaceful, so happy a transit from earth to heaven ! Her sweet spirit was loosed so gently, that the loving watchers knew not the moment of its flight, and would fain believe it still present with them ! Ah ! mercies are inexhaustible ! In the smallest circumstances attending this event, they were most evident ; attesting the protecting care and love of our Heavenly Father, who very tenderly pitieth His children.

We do indeed, with humble and thankful reverence, glorify and praise God that this beloved one is now emancipated from suffering,—that the gates of pain and weakness, of sin and sorrow, are closed behind her for ever,—and that she has entered into the joy of her Lord in mansions of eternal glory! She who was content here on earth to take a lowly place at the feet of Jesus, counting herself unworthy of His inestimable ministry of blessing, has been bidden to "come up higher," even to the seat of His glory, to the "innumerable company of angels" and "the spirits of the just made perfect,"—even to the "church of the firstborn ! "

In the earlier part of her illness she was fearful about herself ; but during my last visit, when speaking of her going to heaven, she said, " I see no reason to doubt it," and was full of the sweet hope and assurance of a blessed eternity. All praise be to Him " who doeth all things well ; " who seeth the end from the beginning, and arrangeth our path in life, each day, as we are able to pursue it.

Two days before her death she said to me, " I wish I could walk ! " little apprehensive, perhaps, how soon she would have her desire realized, and "walk in white " with Jesus.

She was often cheerful, even to mirth ; and sitting near to her,—so that her imperfect speech could be more readily understood,—we had many lively and pleasant conversations. She was frequently visited, in turn, by her children, whom she was always delighted to see ; who derived an affectionate and filial pleasure in her presence, and who "arise up, and call her blessed," besides doubtless many others who have had familiar acquaintance with her. She would say to all who visited her, " God bless you ! " and to her own loved ones, " We shall meet in heaven ! " as if that would quite compensate for all the painful separations here.

As I saw her on her last day on earth, and so many days

previously, with the drooping head and sinking form, and only the dear right hand exerting itself with the power left to it, she forcibly exemplified the sacred injunction, "Whatsoever thy hand findeth to do, do it with thy might."

Her letters were full of power to console, support, revive, and stimulate in the faith and service of our blessed Lord ; also breathing the deepest outpouring of a mother's love, as well as fervent ascriptions of praise and adoration to God for His love and mercy. These reminiscences are her best memorials ; and life-treasures to those who survive her. And surely the prayers they breathed have brought down many blessings from heaven, and laid up treasures there ; having doubtless been the means of drawing the hearts of many to Jesus, and of fixing their affections on things above.

During the last few weeks of her illness, her sleep greatly improved, and her repose at night was correspondingly good, when compared with her former weary, sleepless, restless state, which so greatly distressed her ; and her morning salutation would often be the grateful expression, "Thank God, I have had another good night ! " Thus the Lord tempered her affliction : " He stayeth His rough wind in the day of the east wind," and saith for the solace of His chastened weak ones, " As thy days, so shall thy strength be."

The springs of life being exhausted, she "fell asleep," and awoke with Jesus ! Oh ! wonderful awakening ! Like many others, while standing here in the outer-court of the temple, she would endeavour to penetrate into its inner mysteries, but in vain. But now the veil is rent, and the glory of the inner-court is disclosed to her enraptured vision ; and only the narrow stream of death divides us !

She had long been lingering beside this stream, and we indulged the hope that she might yet be spared to us, until at one step she was carried across into the glorious land !

Thanks be to God, she needs not now to write or talk of Jesus ; seeing Him, as she now does, face to face, and being satisfied for ever in awaking up after His likeness. The end has now come to that wearisome probation, which she bore with such meek humility and patience ; instructing us by her example, and her constant consideration of others, in the midst of her own physical incapacities and sufferings. For her, all the sorrow of the past is departed, and the joy of the present is realized, *never* to depart !

She was remarkable for her fervent piety and domestic virtues. She was beloved by all who knew her, and has left a large circle of relatives and friends to mourn her loss. But our sorrow is buried in her fulness of joy ! Our loss is her eternal gain !

On the last day of her life she heard read with much pleasure the following beautiful lines :

> " Fair is our Promised Land !
>   And gloriously her mansions shine !
> Art thou of Israel's wand'ring band ?
>   Then all that land of light is thine !
>
> On yonder steep hangs high thy crown,
>   There, where the new song now is sung ;
> And He, who cast the angels down,
>   Holdeth for thee a harp new-strung.
>
> Then place thy foot upon the rock,
>   Thy hand upon the promised stay ;
> Fear thou no more the tempest's shock,
>   For none shall rend thy foot away.
>
> Oh ! mount up on faith's radiant wings,
>   Press on the Promised Land to view ;
> Leave thou on earth thy tear-stain'd things,
>   And join the song for ever new.
>
> No more thy hands supinely fold,
>   For ransom'd souls the way have trod :
> Soar up where Jesus led ! Behold
>   The glorious City of our God ! "

My beloved mother's remains were, in accordance with her own request, interred at Wrington, in her husband's grave.

All partings of anguish below,
Will be lost in one meeting above ;
The streamlets that here lonely flow,
There blend in an ocean of love.

A. M. M., Oct. 26, 1874.

MRS. LEEVES,

Widow of the REV. H. D. LEEVES.

Within three months and a-half from the decease of my beloved mother, my dear aunt, Mrs. Leeves, widow of the Rev. H. D. Leeves, Chaplain to H.B.M.'s Legation at Athens, has also departed to her rest ; to join the beloved ones whom she so deeply lamented, and to be "for ever with the Lord," and with the "great multitude" who cry with "a loud voice, saying, Salvation to our God which sitteth upon the throne, and unto the Lamb"—and "blessing, and honour, and glory, and power, be unto Him that sitteth upon the throne, and unto the Lamb for ever and ever."

Mrs. Leeves died of bronchitis, after eight days illness, at Hastings, on the 12th of December, 1874.

Thus has ended this generation of the Leeves family.

A. M. MOON. Jan. 25, 1875.

STRAY THOUGHTS

IN VERSE,

WRITTEN PRINCIPALLY IN EARLY YEARS.

BY

A. M. ELSDALE

(AFTERWARDS MOON).

155

CONTENTS.

K 2

STRAY THOUGHTS.

A Voyage in Greek Waters.

Being a Description of our Passage from Athens to Eubœa, and Journey up
the Country to the Estate of Castaniotissa.

[The following is a brief sketch of a voyage from Athens to Eubœa, by a
family of nine persons, in a Greek ship of war, a " condemned" vessel, as we
afterwards found ; and on one night our danger was great. At night, the
effects of the phosphorescence of the waters beneath, in the ship's wake,
combining with the bright glittering of the stars above, were startlingly beautiful. On landing in Eubœa, we were obliged to stay for the night at a sort of
barn-house. In the morning, we all proceeded to the estate of my uncle (the
Rev. H. D. Leeves), mounted on mules with pack-saddles, attended by the
steward and the guides. We passed through lovely scenery, by bosks of
myrtle, oleanders, etc., anemones of all colours starring and strewing our path.
On reaching the estate, the peasants rushed in a body, with joy, to greet their
lord ("*Affendico*" in Greek) ; and we wound up the hill to the White House,
overlooking the village below, amidst cheers and congratulations.]

We hasten'd from th' Athenian shore,
   That night of matchless light ;
And swiftly rush'd our ship of war
   Over the waters bright,

Cutting the waves in angry din,
   Till o'er its pathway dark
The chafed flood burst in flashing sheen,
   Lighting the fragile bark.

* * *

So sorrow's flood surrounds the Ark
   That wafts us to our rest ;
Yet lights of joy the pathway mark
   Upon its murky breast ;

Like sparks of love struck from the cold
  And flinty heart of man,
Where oft affliction's torrent roll'd
  As swift to joy he ran.

  *   *   *

Thus sprang we hopeless o'er the tide,
  In sickness and despair ;
The roaring sea then open'd wide*
  Its jaws to seize us there !

 * * * *

But now our drooping spirits soar,
  We gaze into the skies ;
Behold ! the whole of heaven's floor
  Glistens with angels' eyes ! †

Beaming in starlight love and glee
  Upon our melting souls,
Thirsting in light with them to flee
  Beyond the gleaming poles,

And dive amidst the cloudland blaze
  Of radiant spotless white,
Floating in robes of shadowy haze
  Amid that pure heav'n's night.

  *   *   *

Evening Prayer on Board Ship.

Our bark glides on, and from its breast
  Ascends the hymn of praise ;
Our fearful spirits hushed to rest,
  A grateful prayer we raise.

---

* It was thought, one night, the vessel could not live through the storm ; and we found afterwards it was a "condemned" vessel ! We were about a week on the voyage.

† The stars at night are inexpressibly beautiful in Eastern climes.

Our souls we place within His hand
  Who steers our bark aright ;
We hasten to another land,
  But keep Him still in sight.

*   *   *

We wake from sleep, and soon appears
  Th' oasis of our rest ;
We land* in smiles that chase our tears,
  And dance † upon its breast.
The gloomy shades steal every ray,
  We cannot reach the goal ;
This night ‡ we must our footsteps stay
  Till darkness' folds unroll.

Night.

In rustic barn we lay us down,
  The fork'd fire darts around ;
" Nay, gentle ladies, do not frown,
  Here peaceful rest is found ! "§
We bake the sweet red eggs and bread,‖
  And then dispense around ;
We hear the Greeks' departing tread,
  And all alone are found.

The little band on bended knees,
  Implore their Father's care ;
And He the grateful incense sees
  From hymns of praises there.

---

* Landing in the island of Eubœa.   † Literal.

  ‡ We could not proceed to the village that evening. They told us, if we did, " the wolves would eat us, or the pirates would take us, or the bandits would seize us," etc.

    § The Greeks said.   ‖ Two days before Easter.

Each weary head inclines to rest,
  The mantle of the night
Spreading its dark and starry vest
  Athwart each vision bright.

　　*　　　　*　　　　*

The Sun Rises,

The shades disperse, and Kate* prepares
  The ever-grateful tea ;
And so dispenses all the " shares,"
  That none for her I see !

　　*　　　　*　　　　*

Mount ! mount ! the mules are all array'd
  With " pack-saddles " to ride ;
And she who feels the most afraid,
  Shall still in safety glide.

The eager rustics seize the rein,
  And on in triumph guide
The smiling ladies, till they gain
  The village of their pride.
They jolt along in mirthful guise,
  Bursting through flood and fell,
Radiant before their sparkling eyes
  The land they love so well !

Ode to Greece.

Sweet Greece ! thy heaven without alloy
  Is like an angel's face,
Transparent to the hues of joy
  That all his features grace !

---

* An inestimable unselfish Swiss " Bonne," whose devoted nursing through
a serious illness was a great means of saving my life.

Sweet Greece ! thy land of magic form
    Is like an angel's wing ;
Be it in sunshine or in storm,
    It gleams a glorious thing !

Thy mountain brows* are clothed in mist,
    A coronet divine,
Which when the glowing sun has kiss'd
    Like golden hills they shine ;
And bathe themselves in changeless rest,
    Fix'd in the depths below,
With smiles upon their peaceful breast
    Midst love's sea's endless flow !

The Peasants' Greeting.

(The peasants coming from the village on the estate, to greet us on our arrival.)

THE peasant train now rush to meet
    The merry, laughing show ;
And throw themselves before his feet
    Their loved " Affendico ! "†
Each swarthy face is wreath'd in smiles,
    Each red hand raised on high ;
Each flower they cull the way beguiles,
    And cheats the weary sigh.

The face of nature beauty wears,
    The earth is fill'd with light ;
And " Diamanti "‡ deck'd appears
    In gold and crimson bright.

---

*A chain of mountains, amongst which are Olympus, Parnassus, etc., we saw from our house in Euboea towering over the azure sea.

†Lord.

‡ The faithful Greek steward of the estate, in jacket of scarlet and gold, and white fustinellos. He was afterwards murdered by some Greeks.

Adown the steep we wind with care,
The dashing torrents cross ;
Safely we pass each pirate snare,
And smile at fear and loss !

The " Affendico's " House.

(First sight of the " Affendico's " House at noon, on a hill, in the midst
of the village.)

FLY I fly!—the White House gleams in sight !
The moss-clad hillocks shine,
The gorgeous stars* our pathway strew,
The land is all divine !
See I " Parádeisos "† waves our way,
The lovely Grecian dame ;
Her dark eyes flashing all she'd say,
Now points our path to fame.

Great "Arab"‡ barks our welcome wild,
And frisks the train to see ;
And gently greets each loving child
That strokes, in fearless glee,
Her white hand o'er his sable back,
And courts his future love
To save her from the robber-pack,
That she may safely rove,

And cull the flowers the livelong day,
And sweetly sleep the night,
Dreaming that morn is come for play,
The merry, dancing wight
Who creeps around her father dear
To steal the frequent kiss,
Her fresh heart glowing deep and clear,
In early gleams of bliss !

---

* Wild anemones. † Her name was, in Greek, " Parádeisos " (Paradise).
‡ An immense black Newfoundland dog.

The Next Morning: Family Prayer: Easter-Day.

" Χριστὸς ἀνέστη ! "—" CHRIST IS RISEN ! "

The Salutation of the Modern Greeks on Easter-day.*

THE morn seems bursting in a blaze !
    As swift they circle round,
And gaze beyond that earth-born haze
    To where their rest is found ;
Beyond that azure peaceful wave,
    Beyond that snowy height,
Where angels' wings their gleamings lave
    In Heaven's eternal light.

Heavenward their grateful souls arise,
    Wing'd by a Father's prayer,†
Exhaled beyond these drooping skies
    And steep'd in glory there ;
Their golden locks glance, glow and gleam,
    Their eyes, undimm'd by tears,
Shine in the floods of light that beam
    On God-giv'n youthful years !

Evening.

(THOUGHTS OF THE FATHER.)

THE hoary head that's blanched for God
    In sorrow's icy wave,
And meekly pales ‡ beneath the rod,
    And sinks into the grave ;

---

* Borrowed from the primitive Christians.

† The Rev. H. D. Leeves, B.D. built, by voluntary contributions, St. Paul's, the first Protestant church at Athens. His father, the Rev. William Leeves, composed the music of " Auld Robin Gray," in 1770.

‡ The father is since dead.

Shall rise in radiance from the tomb,
 In living tints of light,   ·
And rest, for ever past death's gloom,
 On heaven's eternal height !

The glacier gleams in ice and snows,
 Cold, desolate, and lone ; *
In melting sorrows gently flows,—
 Pale death is all her own.
But when the rising sun shall raise
 His gaze to her cold brow,
His glorious hues in streaming blaze
 Of joy shall o'er her flow.

      *   *   *

The wingèd day is past and gone,
 My weary heart seeks rest ;
Not e'en the glorious sun that shone,
 And spread his beauteous vest
Of rosy tints across the sky,
 In mild and dying light,
Gleaming athwart the heavenward eye,
 Like bows of promise bright,   ·

Can stay me from the deep-set rest
 That steeps the peaceful soul,
When thoughts of all that's purest, best,
 Within night's curtains roll.
When, having praised our Father's love,
 His everlasting arms
Enfold us closely from above,
 Secure from earth's alarms !

---

* And afterwards the mother.

LINES

*On seeing a Deaf and Dumb Child, leading a Blind Musician
upstairs to the piano, at Athens.*

HE sweetly smiled, the sightless man,
    Upon the voiceless child,—
As swiftly to and fro she ran,
    In peaceful joy he smiled.
She sat in love beside him there,
    And gazed into his face,
And he would stroke her tresses fair,
    Her classic features trace.

She loved him, for he could not see,—
    He *her*, who could not hear,—
And still in mirth and frolic glee
    Their hearts would draw more near:
And thus, in voiceless intercourse,
    Soothing each other's woe,
In kindly office, mute discourse,
    Sweet *sympathy* they show!

*Ascent to the Drawing-room, with a long trellised Balcony
looking out on the Acropolis.*

*Little M. used to lay her head down on the piano to feel the
vibration.*

Her hand within his strong one clings,
    And draws him forth away,
Then rushing as with angels' wings
    They flying mount, so gay,
That soon they reach the destin'd height ;
    And now she draws him on
To soar in music's magic flight,
    And breathe his soul in song.

Sudden the rush of melody
Pours on the charmèd air,
As white foam o'er the sable rock,
A light amidst despair.
The sparkling stream now leaps along,
Joyous, and bright, and clear,
Now in the mimicry of song *
It dashes wildly there.

Here he begins a piece of music illustrating to the ear, the varying beauties of scenery that we embrace by sight.

The charm'd strain winds through verdant glades,
Surrounds the mountain top ;
Thence trickling through the peaceful shades,
We count each silver drop ;
The stream flows on in changeful mood,
Tranquil, or chaf'd, or gay,
Pouring of joy a glorious flood—
Like nightingales in May.

On, on it glides upon the air
Seizing the sound divine,—
Casting away the waves of care
Where living waters shine ;
It speeds in wild meand'ring way
Into the sea of love,
God's glassy sea in endless day,
Where angels float above :

There, evermore enthroned in light,
The blissful Harper sings
High praise to Him who burst his night,
JESUS—the King of kings !

---

* Mr. T. sang a farmyard song, which he concluded by imitating the Greek singing

He sees, who ne'er on earth could see ;
She hears—her sins forgiven
By Him, who made their sorrows flee,
And waked their souls in heaven !

GENESIS xlv. 26, 27, 28.

"AND JACOB'S HEART FAINTED, FOR HE BELIEVED THEM NOT."

YET *can* it be, that tale
That ye relate to me,
That my wasted eye no more shall bewail
My beautiful and free,
That the cords of life may last,
And the wings of love may fly,
Bearing me on from dark years long past
To see him before I die ?

My heart is flutt'ring faint,
Like a bird on wounded wing ;
O rend not again my sunk soul, to paint
So false, so fair a thing.
My head's with anguish hoary,
In vain ye ceaseless cry
(Now I've wept long years o'er his garments gory)
I shall see him before I die !

Wildly ye still must rave !
Children, where haste ye now ?
Crushed by my sorrows swift down to the grave,
Not to *your* land I go—
Its corn and wine from afar,
Light not my listless eye—
Ah, what vision glides on like a heavenly star—
I *see* him before I die ! *

---

* "And Israel said, It is enough ; Joseph my son is yet alive ; I will go
and see him before I die."—*Gen.* xlv. 28.

THE BLIND CHILD.

A blind child, accustomed to work, had a hard substance grow upon her fingers, which prevented her feeling the embossed reading.* It was removed, but grew again. In farewell sorrow she *kissed* the Book, and found that she could read with her *lips*.

SHE read her Bible o'er and o'er,
　With ever new delight ;
Fill'd with its still increasing store,
　Her faith became her sight.
Ah ! once again those fingers worn
　Refuse to trace the line,
And *thrice* has from her heart been torn
　The page of life divine.

" My God," she cries, in deepest woe,
" I've lost Thy thread of love
In this dark labyrinth below,
　And in the darkness rove !
Who shall assist my failing feet
　And lead me on to Thee,
Where all the angels I may meet,
　And JESUS I may see ? "

She bow'd her head in sorrow meek—
" Thy will be done, O Lord ! "
And sad tears coursing down her cheek,
　She *kiss'd* the Sacred Word.
With lightning flash doth joy inspire
　Her soul, from anguish fled ;
Touch'd with the prophet's coal of fire,
　Her *lips* the Word have read !

Wrington, June, 1849.

---

* This is thought to have been in Dr. Moon's type.

IN ANSWER TO S. L.

On receiving a Rose Leaf on which was written,

"I AM THE ROSE OF SHARON."

' TIS Sharon's Rose, whose gentlest balm
 Sustains the drooping soul ;
Distilling sweet celestial calm
 Where deepest sorrows roll.
The countless fibres of His heart
 Diverge through endless space ;
Twining around the gloomiest part
 Of earth's bewild'ring maze.

      *   *   *

Oh ! may thy gentle heart repose
 Upon thy Saviour's breast ;
Enfolded deep in Sharon's Rose,
 Find there an endless rest !
There may thy soul expand in love,
 There in His image glow ;
And in the Paradise above
 Thy joys eternal flow !

ATHENS.

TO MY FATHER.

VISIONS OF THE PAST.

My father, in this stranger-land, *
 My spirit flies to thee,
Far distant from that happy band
 That crowd and circle thee :

---

* Written at Athens.

L

Oh father, mother, sister, brother,
  The earliest links of love,
In golden strength below no other,
  Fasten'd by cords above.

Father, I see thee where were nursed
  My earliest infant years,
When life's first lovely rosebuds burst,
  Bedew'd with heavenly tears.
I see thee sweetly soothe the spring
  Of life's advancing bloom,
With fragrances of love that bring
  Enchantment through the gloom.

I hear thee charm my couch of pain
  With words of endless life,
Distilling like the gentle rain,
  And chasing earthly strife.
I hear thee heave the painful sigh
  Quick breathing o'er my cheek ;
I see thee raise thy tearful eye,
  And blessings for me seek.*

I see thee leave my silent cell
  Thy echoing footsteps trod,
In anguish seek the peaceful dell,
  And breathe thy soul to God.
Our *heavenly* Father hears thy prayer,
  Thy child is safely kept ;
Her soul is sweetly stay'd from care,
  With joy alone she wept.

*   *   *

* My father prayed by me when ill, and I recovered.

Father, I see thee walk with me
  The Paradise of earth,*
Where ev'ry fresh'ning flow'r and tree
  Still smiles in springing mirth ;
Father, shall we not bless *His* love
  Who spares our peaceful days,
And evermore ascend above,
  In breathings to His praise

Who show'rs His glories on us now,
  Amidst this lovely glade,
And from the threat'ning mountain's brow
  Affords a peaceful shade :
Who spreads the river of His love
  In glist'ning circles round,
And pours from out that warbling grove
  The melody of sound :

Who lands us on this lovely isle †
  To pass our weary way,
And makes our sadden'd hearts to smile,
  And burn with warmest ray,—
The ray of love, that lights the gloom
  Of death, until 'tis heaven ;
The ray that fades not on the tomb,
  By God's own Spirit giv'n ?

*   *   *

My father,—ah ! I see thee now
  Weary, and faint, and pale ; ‡
Thou steadfastly dost raise thy brow
  To Heaven's refreshing gale ;

---

* Our usual Saturday afternoon walk was by a lovely river with an island,
and with verdant banks, trees, rocks, hills, etc., around.

† The river island. ‡ My father was at this time ill in Switzerland.

L 2

Oh list, my father! for the chimes
Of angels * in this night,
When gazing forth in southern climes,
Unutterably bright!

Father, thy fragile suff'ring frame
Is sinking to the tomb,
From whence thy loved and honoured name
Shall still in fragrance bloom.
Translated to Immanuel's land,
In glory shalt thou dwell,
Where may I join the ransom'd band,
With thee I love so well!

There pain and sickness, sorrow, tears,
No more distress the saint,
Whose face in Jesu's likeness wears
That joy no heart can paint.
There prayer is ever merged in praise
From hearts to Jesus given,
Rolling along in endless lays
Throughout the vault of heaven.

MARY'S HUMILITY.

"AND SHE HAD A SISTER CALLED MARY, WHICH ALSO SAT AT
JESUS' FEET, AND HEARD HIS WORD."—*Luke* x. 39.

LORD JESUS! sitting at Thy feet,
Mary her rest did find;
There Thou didst shed Thine influence sweet
Upon her lowly mind.

---

* "Are they not all ministering spirits sent forth to minister for them who
shall be heirs of salvation?"—*Heb.* i. 14.

Lord Jesus! Thou wilt none deny,
  Who seek that peace and rest ;
And those who for Thy presence sigh
  Shall in Thy love be blest.

Lord Jesus! I have often felt
  Thy love inspire my soul ;
Continue, Lord, my heart to melt,
  Under Thy sweet control.

Lord, daily draw my soul away
  From all that tempts below,
Then bear it to Thy heavenly sway
  Where endless pleasures flow.

TO MARY.

IN ANSWER TO VERSES JUST RECEIVED.

I SAW her sweet face gleaming in,
  With all its tones of mirth ;
Her joyous voice would strive to win
  My spirit back to earth.
She calls,—and in her playful glee,
  Would draw me forth away
To follow where her footsteps flee,
  And dance from spray to spray.

With eager care she tends the flowers,
  And drives the dust away ;
And now she weaves her rural bowers,
  And trains the tendril's play.
And constantly she tries to soothe
  My hours of lonely toil,
And the imaginings of youth
  Conveys, to steal a smile.

And what are these sweet lines of prayer *
    Sent to that Saviour dear,
Who makes all those His constant care
    Who seek His love and fear?
That Saviour shall thy prayer attend,
    Breathed in His inmost ear;
Himself shall be thy constant friend,
    And watch thee ever near.

Thy ardent youth He shall control,
    Thy heart from sin release;
And pour into thy rising soul
    The balm of heavenly peace.
And when those golden locks no more
    Dance wildly round thy brow,
A crown of glory,† on death's shore
    Shall be thy locks of snow!

HYMN.

[For Public Worship.]

O Lord, we stand before Thy throne,
    Our fondest wishes pour;
Our hearts Thy heavenly influence own,
    And to Thy presence soar.
The aged and the youthful stand
    In silence at Thy feet,
Upgazing towards that shining land
    Where saints in glory meet.

[Our voices' sweetest harmony
    Now floats upon the air,
Until the dying melody
    Melts in the breath of prayer,

---

* In answer to some verses of prayer. † *Proverbs* xvi. 31.

Sweeping along the quiv'ring strings
  Within our hearts that meet,
And rising now with rapture flings
  High praise before Thy feet.]

Freed by His death from sin's dark thrall,
  We plead before Thy throne
That *Jesus* is our hope, our all,
  And we are His alone :
That all we have in earth or heaven
  We give into His care,
Only desire our sins forgiven
  And in His love a share.

The cords wherewith our hearts are bound
  To those we love, we pray
Let them not twine too closely round,
  Lest they should burst away,
And leave us in our lonely tow'rs
  In this dark world forlorn,
To sorrow for our shelt'ring bow'rs
  Away by tempest torn :

But deep within our meek hearts stamp
  Thy faithful love, O Lord ;
And guide us ever by the lamp
  Of Thy most Holy Word.
Till on the Resurrection-morn,
  Waked from this earthly sleep,
The sun of happiness, new-born,
  Shall drink the clouds that weep,

And then with radiance crown each face
  That erst in tears would gleam,
Gently renew each vanish'd grace
  With his enliv'ning beam ;

When all that ever burn'd before,
  To swell the tide of love,
Wave after wave, on that bright shore,
  Christ's praise shall roll above !

TO MARY.

In answer to verses received.

My heart's in heaven, the flow'rs of earth
  For me are faded long ;
Its tones of joy have fled away,
  Not here I'd tune my song :

I'd take my harp with ransomed saints,
  All glist'ning with delight ;
Their hearts outgushing waves of song,
  As warriors * rest from fight.

Their silver notes steal through my soul,
  Echoing amidst the stars ;
Swelling and sinking as they roll
  To heaven's remotest bars.

Their wings they close around them now,
  Weigh'd by excess of glory ;
Prostrate they sink before His feet,
  Breathing the wondrous story,—

" 'Worthy the Lamb ! ' † who died for us,
  That we might live with Him ;
Who laid His glories in the dust,
  Whose eyes with tears were dim :

---

* " There remaineth therefore a rest to the people of God."—*Heb.* iv. 9.
† Song of the Redeemed.—*Rev.* v. 9.

" That He might brighten all our days
  In life's cold languid vale ;
Tracing along His snowy path,
  To where the end we'd hail

" The golden gates that open'd wide,
  The spirits bright that staid
To greet us rising from the tide,
  Where late o'erwhelm'd we laid ! "

        *   *   *

And, now, amazed, I meet thee there !
  Our liquid harps we ring,
Trickling in lucid notes of peace,
  Like drops beneath a spring.

The chords with ecstasy we strike,
  And join the glorious cloud
Of saints redeem'd unto the Lamb,
  Heaven's concave echoing loud !

TO MARY.

NIGHTLY * now it welcomes me,
  That billet from afar ;
Gleaming in light upon my sight,
  Constant as evening star.

Retiring at the close of day,
  With strength and hope depress'd,
Its thoughts of peace refresh my soul
  Before I sink to rest.

---

* We carried on at this time a daily correspondence in verse.

Ah! what are these memorials fair,
Which thou hast sent to me ?—
Roses, and crowns, and lilies there,
And a ship * that skims the sea.

Oh! may our bark glide peaceful on,
Thus dancing o'er the tide,
Till moor'd in port, with roses twined
And lilies, which we've sigh'd

To bind around our yearning brows;
But still the wreath would fall,
The thorn would steal the drops of pain
In beauty's magic hall!

*   *   *

But, lo! the piercing thorns are gone,
And who hath drawn them forth ?—
See them infix'd in Jesu's brow,
Streaming in drops of wrath!

Lord Jesus! is it Thou that steal'st
Away our wreaths of pain!
Oh! cast the sorrows from Thy brow,
And take Thy crown again!

Lord Jesus! raise our grateful love
Beyond heaven's highest hills;
Then crown us with eternal truth,
And joy that seraphs fills!

---

* A drawing sent with the verses.

O LORD MY ROCK.

"Unto Thee will I cry, O Lord my Rock."—*Psalm* xxviii. 1.

To Thee I cry, O Lord my rock!
When sinks my soul in woe;
Oh! raise me by Thy sure support
Where streams of mercy flow.
To Thee I cry, O Lord my Rock!
When clouds and tempests rise;
·Be Thou my everlasting trust,
And wipe my weeping eyes.

To Thee I cry, O Lord my Rock!
When lurid lightning glares,
And all the lonely blasted pines
In dreadful fury tears!
To Thee I cry, O Lord my Rock!
And, shelter'd by Thy arms,
My spreading branches safely rest,
And smile, secure from harms.

        *   *   *

To Thee I sigh, O Lord my Rock!
In panting heat my shade;
Enclosed in Thee, I taste the sweets
Whose freshness doth not fade.
To Thee I sigh, O Lord my Rock!
When faint with dying thirst;*
And from Thy tender bosom's store
The living waters burst!

        *   *   *

---

* "They drank of that spiritual Rock that followed them: and that Rock was Christ."—1 *Cor.* x. 4.

To Thee I cry, O Lord my Rock !
When storms of grief descend ;
The angry billows vainly roll,
My Saviour and my Friend.*
For I am still entwined with Thee,
Above, beneath, around ;
The ivy clings unto her rest,
And there her strength is found.

To Thee I cry, O Lord my Rock !
When death's dark stream is near ;
And gently raised above the wave,
My heart rests calmly there.
To Thee I cry, O Lord my Rock !
And life's short tempest o'er,
Its floods and storms are all forgot,
Lost on that peaceful shore !

TO MARY.

AN ANSWER.

DAILY my prayers to heaven ascend,
For thee, my loved, my youthful friend,
In wakeful, silent sympathy.

With other loved ones thee I'd bear
Above, beyond these waves of care ;
Which, rising still with eager haste,
Would lave away the path we've traced
To guide us hourly nearer heaven.

*   *   *

---

* *Psalm* xix. 14.

But still the rainbow, midst our fears,
With peaceful olive-branch appears,
    Reposing calmly o'er the flood.

Faith has the infant's guileless eye,
Adoring still with happy sigh
The mother where its hopes are placed,
With tender smiles and beauty graced,
    Through ev'ry changing hurricane.

EASTER DAY.

THE virgin Moon reflects her light
    Upon our darkling earth,
Peaceful and silent, mantling night
    With gleams of heavenly mirth.

So the pure Jesus walked in light
    Amidst our souls in shade,
Casting before th' illumined sight
    Th' eternal ransom paid.

His soul was stay'd in mountain-air,
    Fast by the throne of God ;
While oft the wrestling midnight prayer
    Embalm'd the path He trod.

His Father heard him from the mist
    Of glory where He sat ;
And there were angels who would list,
    And flee to soothe His state.

        *   *   *

Methinks I hear a spirit-voice
    Carolling from the tomb ;
It says, " Rejoice, O still rejoice !
    The flowers freshly bloom.

"The 'Rose of Sharon' blooms this day
    In th' Paradise of God ;
And grateful odours charge the way
    From incense of His blood!

"The 'cloud of witnesses' proclaim
    The song in earth and heaven :
'Glory for ever to the Lamb
    Who hath our ransom given !

" 'Who shines in love into our hearts,
    And draws them close to Him ; '
While seraph-angels take their parts,
    And laud with cherubim."

SEPARATION.

I PRAY to my Father in heaven,
    When my soul is deep-sinking in woe ;
And the streams of His mercy are given,
    As a full heart before Him doth flow.

I spread all my sorrows around,
    Like a sable cloud hiding the sun ;
And when I my Saviour have found,
    He smiles, and my course I still run.

    *   *   *

I gather my loved ones with me
    In spirit to kneel round the throne,
Its light and its glory to see,
    Like sweet birds from earth that have flown.

Encircling there still we ascend
    In earnest desires of our rest,
Till our hearts in full-unison blend
    In the joyous abodes of the blest.

There, raised far above space and time,
  Earth's cold bars no longer shall sever ;
For, once fled to that happy clime,
  We know we shall love there for ever !

*   *   *

All partings of anguish below,
  Will be lost in one meeting above ;
The streamlets that here lonely flow,
  There blend in an Ocean of Love !

"SHE'S GONE !"

(A SISTER'S LAMENT.)

Her full dark eye would rest on mine,
  In calm and peaceful love ;
Then raised to heaven, again would shine
  With radiance from above.
So clear and bright it glisten'd there,
  It seem'd like lucid well,
Wherein we see reflected fair
  The stars in heaven's cell.

It drank the purest lights above,
  In ardent, wistful gaze ;
Then shed them down in looks of love
  Fresh caught from Jesu's face :
Casting resplendent gleams around
  Upon the watchful throng,
She pour'd her richest joys in sound
  In tones of heavenly song.

Her soul was pierced by sorrow's sting,
  Too gentle for this earth ;
But still she would to Jesus cling,
  And he hath drawn her forth,

And placed her where the tears that stood
　Still quiv'ring in that eye
Are quenched for ever, in the flood
　Of joy that dwells on high !

　　　*　　　　*　　　　*

[*The departed spirit speaks from heaven !*]

From heaven she speaks, " Oh sister dear,
　Lift up thy streaming eye ;
Behold me filled with glory here !—
　And thus forget to sigh.
Our sweetest converse, happiest, best,
　Was but to long for heaven ;
Then, why lament ?—at last I rest
　Where all my heart was given !

" Mother and sister ! swift as light
　The moments hasten on ;
Soon shall ye walk in robes of white,
　With me, beside the throne !
There shall you bless the wondrous love
　That raised me first to glory ;
Like wreath of snow exhaled above,
　Not blanch'd with sorrows hoary ! "

EARLY REMEMBRANCES.

The fairest forms of early youth
　Now flit before mine eye ;
In all their sweetest love and truth
　In childhood's mirth they fly.

The merry games and infant plays
　That pleased (we knew not why),
Crowded around our early days
　Before we learnt to sigh.

The fleeting beat of youthful feet
That danced along the floor,
And rushed away with joy to greet
Sweet Susan* at the door.

With joyous chime did sweet young time
His merry bells ring out ;
As wild with sparkling glee we'd climb
The Simshill's dewy " tout." †

The smiles, the tears, of those bright years,
We mingled there together ;
Nor ever glanced at parting fears,
Nor dreamt of wintry weather.

The summer birds that sang aloft,
The strawberries that grew ;
Where oft we made our couch so soft,
Where the pink heather blew.

The village bells, with silvery tongue,
That chimed upon the ear ;
We on their accents startled hung,—
" Is't joy or grief we hear ? "

These memories rest in thankful hearts
Close-linked in early love ;
And when the tear of sadness starts,
We raise our thoughts above

To *Him*, who dwelt upon our earth,
Weigh'd by excess of sorrow ;
Who *died* to give us heavenly birth,
And life a brighter morrow !

---

* One of my companions in childhood.
† In Somersetshire a hill is sometimes called a tout.

M

A SISTER'S MARRIAGE.

(AFTER OUR FATHER'S DEATH.)

My father! see thy children-band
　Gliding in robes of white
Slow past thy tomb, whilst thou dost stand
　In heaven's effulgent light.

And canst thou blessings on us pour
　As thou didst here on earth,
And raise our trusting spirits more
　To climes where joy has birth?

Blest *are* we, in our Home above,
　We have *two* Fathers now
Gazing with more than earthly love
　Upon each changing brow.

　　　*　　　*　　　*

God of our life! who guid'st us o'er
　This pathway to the skies,
Preserve the *loved one* who no more
　Amidst us smiles or sighs.

Crown her with blessings that belong
　To those Thou lovest best;
Then waft her, midst th' angelic throng,
　To Thine eternal rest!

WRINGTON.

A FAREWELL.

To A. M. E., *on going to Argos.*

We part, my Anna, e'en to-morrow,
　And wilt thou often think of me ?
Oh ! when thy heart is full of sorrow,
　Oh ! then, my love, remember me !

And when thou with another sing'st
　The songs that I have sung with thee ;
And when thou with another walk'st,
　Oh ! then, my love, remember me !

And when thou'rt in the moonlight roaming,
　And gazing on the placid sea ;
And when on past scenes thou art musing,
　Oh ! then, my love, remember me !

Oh ! when thy heart is sad and sair,
　And oceans roll 'twixt me and thee,
Then, at the mercy-seat of prayer,
　Oh ! *there*, my love, remember me !

　　　　　　　　　　　　　　M. A. L.
Athens.

TO A. M. E.

*On leaving Athens for England.**

My Anna, take this pledge of love,
　And wear it long for me :
And ever may thy passage here
　Gentle and happy be.

---

* With a parting present.

M 2

May sparkling health around thee fly,
  And love thy path adorn ;
Sweet Hope her freshest flow'rets strew
  O'er each returning morn.

May Peace thy raven tresses twine,
  And blessings o'er thee shed,
And angel-like in mercy stand
  Beside thy dying bed.

And when to Albion's lovely land
  Thy home-sick footsteps flee,
Still wander to a southern strand,
  And sometimes think of me.

Still let thy thoughts, in lonely hours,
  O'er oceans wing their flight,
And Athens flit across the scene,
  Bathed in its sunny light.

And when at last thy race is run,
  And thou hast reached the goal,
May angels hover round thy couch,
  Receive thy parting soul.

                  M. A. L.

LATER

STRAY THOUGHTS.

I LOVE THE LORD.

I LOVE the Lord, who changeth not
(I know He loves us best *)—
All other friends will pass away,—
In *Him* I'll take my rest !

The flood of Jesu's love alone
Can lave my griefs away ;
As wrecks upon a desert shore,
In mem'ry's sunset ray.

Engulf'd beneath that priceless sea,
They sink in caverns lost ;
While crystal sparkles, pearly gems,
Are to the surface tossed :

Jewels, that lie deep down below
The world's remotest ken ;
The tears of penitence and love
That rise to Christ again.

With Him I'll sail on that deep flood,
Wafted in endless peace ;
His sun to shine, His hand to steer,
Till shades and breakers cease.

1863.

---

* "We love Him because He first loved us."—1 *John* iv. 19.

ANSWERS TO VALENTINES FROM MY HUSBAND.

FEBRUARY 14, 1867.

To thine, my faithful heart responds,
In love's entrancing stable bonds;
May Hymen's deep-set golden chains
Be surely everlasting gains,

Winding around our path on earth,
Symbols of constancy and worth;
Till links of love no more we need,
Where love in essence reigns indeed!

FEBRUARY 14, 1868.

AN answ'ring note thy lyre requires
Of warm and tender love,
Breathing amidst the dewy spires
As coos the whisp'ring dove;

Mounting above these rugged plains
To lands of golden light,
Where, joined eternally, He deigns
To fill us with delight.

Before the throne of God, our Lord,
The past shall stand out clear,
Traced in light by the glorious Word
Who brings us safely there.

Ecstatic praise shall then reveal
The souls so clouded here,
As long-imprisoned waters steal,
And rainbow tints appear.

Then shall the river of our joy
In widening courses rove,
Time's shifting waves of past alloy
Merge in that Sea of Love.

ON MY MOTHER'S DEATH.

FAITH's rainbow on the sombre cloud
Of death, gleams forth (how beauteous both !)
While choirs of angels sing aloud :
"To give thy loved one be not loth,
We bear her hence to realms of light,
Where Jesu's love for ever reigns ;
There, clad in glistening robes of white,
To swell His praise in heavenly strains."

My sainted mother comes to me
In visions sweet and thoughts of night,
Once more, in fancy, I can see
Her loving eyes, in lustre bright.
Once more, I hear the blessings deep
That welled forth from her steadfast heart,
That caused me both to smile, and weep
The blessed tears where joy hath part.

'Twas sorrow streaked with rays of glory
Poured from the heaven to which she sped,
'Twas joyous faith in Scripture story
That death is life, *with Christ* our Head !
My mother ! in these later years,
The cord that bound us was of love
So closely drawn, entwin'd with fears
Lest death should let thy spirit rove

To realms supernal, far from me !
That, when thy happy soul had fled,
No light in darkness could I see ;
    And every joy to me was dead—
Where was thy sweet enshrining love ?
    A mother's wing spread o'er her child !
The love we prize not till we rove
    Midst thorny brakes, and deserts wild !

Oh, pour thy griefs in Jesu's ear,
    He *knows* them all, but will be *told*—
He loves thy trusting voice to hear,
    He sympathizes, as of old—
He thus poured out strong cries and tears,
    He succours all who do the same,
For He our human nature wears
    Nor is our Friend alone in *name*.

Oh, then, gird up thy loins again,
    He'll be thy staff, thy strength, thy stay ;
He'll never let thee brave in vain
    The toils and dangers of the way.
He'll daily wash thy bleeding feet
    In precious blood He shed for thee,
Until thou'rt quite prepared to meet
    With all thou wouldst rejoice to see !

*　　　*　　　*

When stringent anguish racks the nerve
    Enfeebled by successive blows,
Oh, never from thy Saviour swerve
    Who sees and mitigates thy woes.
He holds the iron that doth strike
    Into thy soul with searching power ;·.
And faith should rest on Him, alike
    In days of ease and sorrow's hour.

[He knows thy frame, and sees thy grief,
  For He knew every mortal pain ;
His loving hand will give relief,
  And cleanse thy soul from every stain.]
And when the crashing strokes have rent
  Each lingering sin, each earthly love,
In desolation—Heaven-sent—
  The Christian seeks his rest above.

Death's final blow then Jesus gives,*
  The mercy-stroke to still his pain ;
And where the Lord for ever lives
  He bears him, to revive again :
With songs of rapture to adore
  The love that ne'er from Him would part,
And keeps him still for evermore
  Clinging to Jesus, heart to heart !

     *   *   *

Oh, Saviour ! grant my mother's prayer
  So often steeped in flowing tears,
Addressed to Him she knew would hear,
  And scatter all her anxious fears :
† "Lord, bring my children to Thy seat
  Of peace, and joy, and perfect love !
Oh Jesu ! grant we all may meet—
  One family, in Heaven above ! "

A. M. M.,

1874.

---

  * The last, or death-blow on the wheel, was called by the French the
" *Coup de grace.*"
        † The substance of my mother's prayer.

MY MOTHER.

[Written on the Day of my beloved Mother's Funeral.]

AND can I truly think she's gone,
    And borne away her love ;
And left me weeping here alone,
    To dwell with God above !
Her words, in time of earthly ruth,
    Have rapt me to the skies,
Burning, with all their joy and truth,
    The tears from weeping eyes.

Her hand, which toiled in weakness brave,
    These lovely thoughts to trace,
Now lies in peace within the grave,
    For she has run her race,—
She's passed the scorching desert through *
And made a dip in death,
To rise, in gardens ever new,
    When she resigned her breath.

The joys and ecstasies above
    We cannot grudge her now,
But still rejoice that there she'll rove,
    No sadness on her brow ;
But ever beaming with delight,
    She'll dwell amidst the stars,
Soaring, in all their glorious light,
    To heaven's remotest bars.

---

* "The River Guadalquiver passes through a desert, then makes a dip
under the ground, and rises again in a beautiful luxuriant valley."

LINES

Written for my beloved, numerous " Collectors," who commenced August 21st, 1880, to take cards to collect 10s. each, for the Irish Society (Bruey Branch).

LORD, send Thy Word to Erin's isle
 In her loved *native* tongue,*
Thus, all her sorrows to beguile,
 While songs of joy are sung.
Jesus, the Light of all the world
 Come down and chase the gloom ;
For where Thy standard is unfurl'd
 Peace, love, and joy shall bloom.

United by Thy mighty sway,
 We join the League of Love †
Which, long years past, has led the way
 To Thy bright courts above.
Lord, hold us in Thy powerful hand,
 And bear us on our way,
A happy, joyous, prayerful band—
 We have no *other* stay !

Oh, give us, Lord, some thousand souls
 To learn, and do Thy will ;
And, as the Gospel river rolls,
 May we, unwearied still,

---

* According to the Census of 1861, more than one million of the people of Ireland spoke the Irish language, of whom 163,000 were returned as not speaking English. Through the operations of the Irish Society for the last fifty years, at least 150,000 Irish-speaking people have been taught to read the Holy Scriptures in their own tongue. It costs only 15 shillings to have one poor Irish person taught to read.—*Report.*

† The Irish Society was established in 1818.

Pour in the tributary streams
　To swell the glorious tide,
Till, in the ocean of our dreams—
　Thy love, we e'er abide !

Lord, touch our lips with prophet's fire
　To speak Thy healing name,
And satisfy our heart's desire
　That *all* may grasp the same.
Let sad Hibernia slake her thirst
　At living streams divine,
Her galling chains of error burst—
　And all the praise be Thine !

Then, Liberty indeed she'll find
　Wherewith the *Lord* makes free,
His servant rest, with willing mind,
　To whom we bow the knee
And praise Him in continual love,
　For all His boundless grace,
Until we dwell with Him above,
　And see Him face to face !

So, Erin's Harp,* that rests above,
　Thron'd on the clouds of night,
Strung by the mighty power of love,
　Wakes in her *Sun-Dawn Light !* †
And rings the echoes of her past
　To boundless praise and joy
Reaching, in circling waves, at last
　To spheres without alloy !

A. M. MOON, *Hon. Sec.,*
Central Brighton Branch,

OCTOBER 16TH, 1880.

---

* This refers to Ireland's emblem ; a harp resting on dark clouds, and the sun rising in glory behind it, dispersing the clouds.

† " But unto you that fear My name, shall the Sun of righteousness arise with healing in His wings."—MAL iv. 2.

A PRAYER FOR IRELAND.

LORD ! soothe our Erin's throbbing breast,
Her aching heart lay still,
And calm the waves of deep unrest
Within Thy holy will !
Lord, walk upon the turbid sea
Of human thoughts and fears,
And tread it down, till love to Thee
Is pressed from all its tears ;

Till rainbow hopes athwart the cloud
Ethereal beauty throw,
And, loving echoes sound aloud
From *God*, we long to know !
And with His promise in our path,
To guide our heavenward way,
Our hearts shall leap for joy, in faith
To see His glorious *Day !* *

The Heaven of rest dawns on our view
With golden harps new-strung,
Where weary souls shall chant anew,
With never faltering tongue,
The endless record of *Thy* pain
Who *died* their life to save
And bear them up with Thee to reign,
Victorious o'er the grave ?

May *Erin's* future rise above
The dark impending gloom,
And halcyon days of peace and love
In radiance o'er her loom.

---

* " Looking for and hasting unto the coming of the day of God."
2 *Peter* iii. 12.

Lord, raise her early Church to shine,*
Revived by God's pure Word,†
Effulgent in its light divine
And Spirit-piercing sword !

A TRIP TO HORSMONDEN.

MAY 19, 1881.

A GLORIOUS morn salutes our eyes,
    As filled with hope and joy we rise,
And wend our way from Tunbridge Wells
Midst lovely hills, and flowery dells.
Horsmonden we reach at last
    Where Dr. Moon‡ revives the past,
And shows the house where he was born
    One bright, auspicious, fateful morn.

He mounts the stairs, and treads the floor
Where first his infant features wore
A smile of innocent delight,
    Inspired by Heavenly fancies bright.
He prays, and thanks the God of love
    For all His mercies from above,
For this existence He has given
    To last eternally in Heaven !

---

* "In 1135, Pope Adrian (the Englishman) issued a bull granting to Henry 11. lordship of Ireland on condition that he would *force the Irish Church to conform to the Church of Rome, then Papal,* and oblige every family to pay one penny to St. Peter and the Holy See. Henry conquered, and *with the sword forced the Roman Catholic religion on the Irish people."* —IRELAND—PAST, PRESENT, AND FUTURE. Gleanings from History. By A. M. L.

† The "Irish Society," established in 1818, gives the people the Bible in the Irish language, and teaches them to read it.

‡ Inventor of Moon's system of Reading for the Blind ; himself blind.

It may be, in some future day
When we shall all have passed away,
That men shall say, here rose the *Moon*
'Who gave the Blind that glorious boon,
To read, with speed by *fingers' ends*
The same as sight to numbers lends !
Therefore, we'll hope that *Moon*-light pleasures
May span the globe in circling treasures !

The Norman church with tower square,
Still gives the scene a sacred air
Where, dedicated to the Lord,
William* has heard His holy Word.
While Addie trips the bright green sward,
The cuckoo's plaintive tone is heard
Reminding us, hopes rise again
From years not wholly spent in vain.

The park is strewn with oaks and elms,
Where beauty all the landscape whelms ;
Water and wood, sun glancing beam
And happiness around us gleam.
The bluebell studs the grassy mound,
I seize and press it, as if found
The youthful hopes that melt away
And vanish, like the dreams of day.

The lovely flower brings back to view
Sweet childhood's days, when all was new
We plucked it, azure as the skies,
Enraptured with its glorious dyes ;
We felt that it was fresh from Heaven,
A link thereto, and therefore given
To weld our souls to worlds above,
And bind our hearts in perfect love.

---

* Dr. Moon's Christian name.

N

Goudhurst we reach, and there have tea,
A hav'n of rest is found for me,
While they explore this pleasant land
Where children sport, a happy band.
In easy Landau we return,
While swelling hearts within us burn
To see the Spring with opening charms
Embrace all nature in her arms.

To Lamberhurst and Pembury
Through lanes embow'red in trees we fly,
And, as we linger midst the vale,
Sweet early mem'ries swell the tale.
We reach our home, and praise the Lord
For all His peace, and all His Word,
With rest and joy dispensed to those
Who in his grace and love repose.

Through life's journey, warp and woof *
Of prayer and answer, form a proof
Of mighty love from God to man,
According with His wondrous plan
To make us lean, like bending reed
Upon His stronghold in our need,
His refuge for our souls to claim,
And trust our all on His great name !

Sion House, Mount Sion.
MAY 19th, 1881.

---

* This idea was taken from a Sermon of the Rev.—Townsend, Trinity
Church, Tunbridge Wells.

EVENING PRAYER.

JESUS ! I lean upon Thy breast,
My sure, and only lasting stay ;
I *pray* Thee give me perfect rest,
And strength still equal to my day :
A rest in *Thee*, for none beside
Can smooth life's rugged, devious way,
And let me not stray far and wide
From Thee, the glorious Light of day !

Oh, let me cling unto my rest
And lay my heavy burden down,
For Thou, Lord, knowest what is best,
To bear "the cross before the crown."
And can I ever hope to wear
A crown of joy in Heaven above ?
Yea, Lord, for Thou my sins didst bear,*
And Thy eternal name is *Love*! †

Sion House, Mount Sion.
MAY 19th, 1881.

LINES

Written on the Evening of a day spent at Plumpton (12 miles from Brighton) by Dr. Moon and friends, St. Swithin, July 15th, 1881.

A friend of days long past, said, "Write some lines ; "
For we shall pass from Brighton's bliss, to mines
Of wealth and beauty, raised above the sod
By the all-fructifying hand of God !

---

* Isaiah liii. 4, 5,   † ." I and My Father are one."—*John* x. 30.

N 2

We braved the heat, and rested in the shade,
While flutt'ring breezes on our scorched brows played
Like dreams of Eden, mixed with this world's glare,
An under-current to the sad and sair.

The village gained, we find our friends of old
Charmed to revive the ties of mortal mould ;
While illness and affliction clear the sight
Which pierces to the Heavenly realms of light—
Now seize the rays of joy, while mirth prevails,
And love and happiness e'er swell the sails
Of each calm vessel, gliding o'er time's sea
Swift to the ocean of eternity !

The day is passed, as other days on earth,
With more or less of joy, and peace, and worth ;
We homeward drive, by beauty's chosen route,
While of the morning's heat we reap the fruit.
Bless'd breezes steal o'er fevered frame and mind,
So softly blows the whispering, cooling wind
Breathing of heavenly airs, and joys complete
When Christ, and all our loved ones we shall meet !

The Downs' soft outlines rise before our view,
Em'rald and harmonious, while the dew
Sinks in the bosom of each lonely hill
Scarred by time's rocks, and pierced by trickling rill.
Faintly, in distance, dawns old Hayward's Heath
A crest of clouds of gorgeous hues beneath :
Clouds that are building up a heavenly site,
While flecks from angels' wings seem tears of light.

The pedestrian trio mount the hill,
While *Moon*-light* in the carriage resteth still.
Entranced with nature's face in evening shades,
We linger midst the deep green, velvet glades.

* Dr. Moon remained in the barouche.

Alderney cows in dusky beauty file,
Their loving, liquid eyes meet ours the while.
Arborous majesty, in Park of Paine,
Suggests, in this fair spot calm joys should reign.

How sweet the prospect of that glorious time
When *all* shall render to the *Great Sublime*
Ecstatic love and praise, swelling the heart,
Whelming the mem'ry of earth's keenest dart.
To be immersed in *God*, and one with Him,
That only, fills our cup, beyond the brim
O'erflowed with joy supreme : rays from *His* Sun,
We must be gathered into *Him*, in one.

Eleven Fanes, arise on our brief way,
Blessing the landscape, as they peaceful lay
Pointing to heaven—with slender, piercing spires
Calling to the angels' rapturous quires !
Brighthelmstone gained, with grateful hearts for all
God's mercies past, for *more* to Him we call !
And mem'ry paints the joyance of the way
That notched time's shining wing, this brilliant day !

LINES

*Written on the Visit of Their Royal Highnesses, The Prince and
Princess of Wales, to Brighton, to open the Children's Hospital,
July 21st, 1881.*

ALBERT, our Royal Prince, illumes the way,
And sheds delight and beauty o'er the day !
All hearts arise to greet him, and to bring
Affection's tribute to our future King !
As heart of one, now stirs the mighty crowd,
Bursting with joy and acclamations loud ;
A sea of heads whose waves retire in love,
To let our gracious Prince pass on above

The hill, where suffering children wait his glance
And kindly words, more famed than deeds of lance ;
While his fair Princess, lovely and beloved,   .
Met Danish flag where'er her eye hath roved ;
While Union Jack and Royal Standard float
As formerly, above some ancient moat,
And wave our love and welcome to his feet,
Who comes his future people's sight to meet

Bedimmed with silvery tears,—while golden prayers
Rise to the *Prince of Peace*, who ever rears
His altar in the hearts of all who give
Their souls into His care, and bids them live !
Lord, give our England's Prince Thy love and grace
To follow Thee, through life's bewildering maze,
To bear us up, on steadfast throne of peace,
Till throughout all the world sad wars shall cease :

Till brotherhood around the globe shall meet,
And earth's domains become Thy glorious seat
All nations' flags unite in one great joy,
No widow's tears the rapture to alloy.
Meanwhile, *Victoria's* throne establish fast,
Our *gracious Queen*,—Lord, grant her life may last
Long years, enshrined in purest happiness,
Till changed earth's crown for one of heavenly bliss !

The sun has fled ! the evening shades prevail,
Illumination tells her wondrous tale
In loving characters of living light,
Piercing the night of time with future sight,
" God bless our brave, kind-hearted Prince of Wales,"
" Albert and Alexandra."   In the scales   .
Of " health and happiness," may they weigh down
The beam of sorrow,—be their people's crown

Of joy! and so illume the British throne,
That shining o'er the earth it may be known,
Spreading its wings to succour the distressed,
Bearing the shield of God upon its breast !
O blest and happy day now past—Adieu !
We've seen the streams of loyal love, anew
Rise to a flood, sweeping down time's rough banks,
While England's Volunteers e'er swell their ranks !

The young Princesses with their parents came,
Nor found their love and kindness but a name :
Reared in such school—grandsire, Albert the Good,
May peace and joy o'erflow them like a flood !
May satisfaction all their steps attend,
And God direct their path unto the end
Of life's short journey—till in heavenly rest
They find, above, *God's* glory is the best !

SCEPTICISM.

Though mud and dirt into the well of Truth
False sceptics throw, with neither fear nor ruth,
Soon the water settles, seeming clearer,
While raised by mire beneath to Heaven *nearer !*

TO

W. MOON, LL.D.,

ON HIS

BIRTHDAY, DEC. 18th, 1886.

———

Dr. Moon's System of Reading for the Blind, invented by himself in 1845, is now embossed in 350 languages.

———•———

Friend of the Blind! thy light has come
  On this auspicious day;
A year still nearer to thy *Home,*
  On life's bewild'ring way.
Thy times are in thy Father's hands,
  He guides thy path aright,
And leads thee past time's shifting sands
  To hail *His* glorious light !

And light thou *giv'st* unto the Blind
  To read God's Holy Word;
For fingers' touch unsheathes to mind
  *The "Spirit's" trenchant "Sword" !
Long may'st thou hold this glorious course,
  Trampling on sin and shame;
Revealing unto all, the source
  Whence comes the great "*new name !*"

---

* "The sword of the Spirit which is the Word of God."—Eph. vi. 17.

From Christ our *Sun*, thou hast the light
  Reflected all around ;
Like the fair planet of the night
  That moves without a sound :
Like her, may'st thou absorb *His* love
  Who fills the worlds, and space ;
For love is light, where e'er we rove,
  Effulgent in *His* face !

And when, at last, thy race is run,
  And Birthdays disappear
Absorb'd in the sweet words " Well done " !—
  This sounds as clarion clear
" Enter thy Lord's great joy " above,
  Where sin and sorrow cease,
And dwell in *Everlasting Love*,
  And God's eternal peace !

A. M. MOON.

DR. MOON'S TYPE FOR THE BLIND.

"This Type was invented by DR. MOON in 1845, and has since been adapted by him to 350 languages and dialects. The alphabet consists of nine characters only, and is suitable for all languages. The number of volumes embossed in this type up to July 1887, has been 168,000, and readers of these books may be found in almost every civilized country in the world, indeed it may be said that the sun never sets upon them. The entire Bible in English, and portions in each of the other languages have been embossed, besides Histories of England, Scotland, ancient Rome and Greece, Assyria, Babylon, Persia, Egypt, and Syria; also a considerable amount of Biography, Poetry, Natural History, a Biblical Dictionary, a General Dictionary, and a large number of religious works, including the Pilgrim's Progress, the Scotch Metrical Psalms and Paraphrases. The list of these embossed books is daily increasing and the number of readers which now amounts to many thousands, is daily increasing also. Maps Geographical and Astronomical, Pictures, Diagrams, and many other things DR. MOON has had embossed for the Blind, as well as providing them with the means of writing both for their blind and sighted friends.

It would be impossible to estimate the value and comfort the books have been to the Blind, and to many not only blind, but deaf and dumb. More than half the readers are over 50 years of age; many are 80, and some are above 90 years."

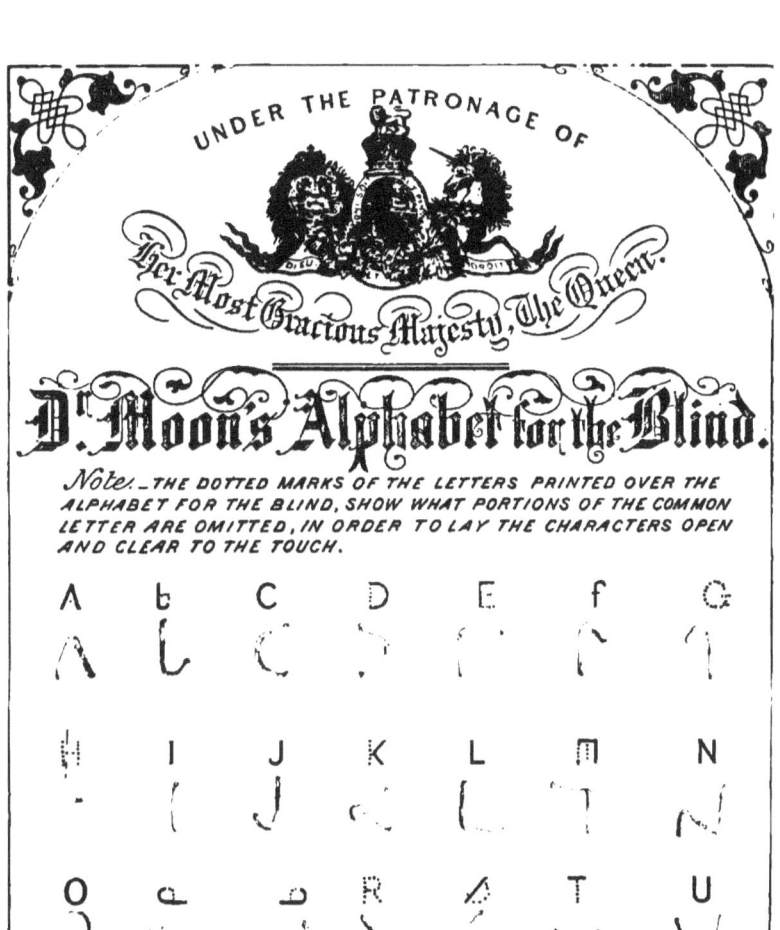

UNDER THE PATRONAGE OF

Her Most Gracious Majesty, The Queen.

Dr. Moon's Alphabet for the Blind.

Note: —THE DOTTED MARKS OF THE LETTERS PRINTED OVER THE ALPHABET FOR THE BLIND, SHOW WHAT PORTIONS OF THE COMMON LETTER ARE OMITTED, IN ORDER TO LAY THE CHARACTERS OPEN AND CLEAR TO THE TOUCH.

A B C D E F G

H I J K L M N

O P Q R S T U

V W X Y Z &

GOD IS LOVE

THE ABOVE ALPHABET CONSISTS OF EIGHT OF THE ROMAN LETTERS UN-ALTERED, FOURTEEN OTHERS WITH PARTS LEFT OUT, AND FIVE NEW AND VERY SIMPLE FORMS, WHICH MAY BE EASILY LEARNED BY THE AGED, AND PERSONS WHOSE FINGERS ARE HARDENED BY WORK.

104, QUEEN'S ROAD, BRIGHTON, SUSSEX.

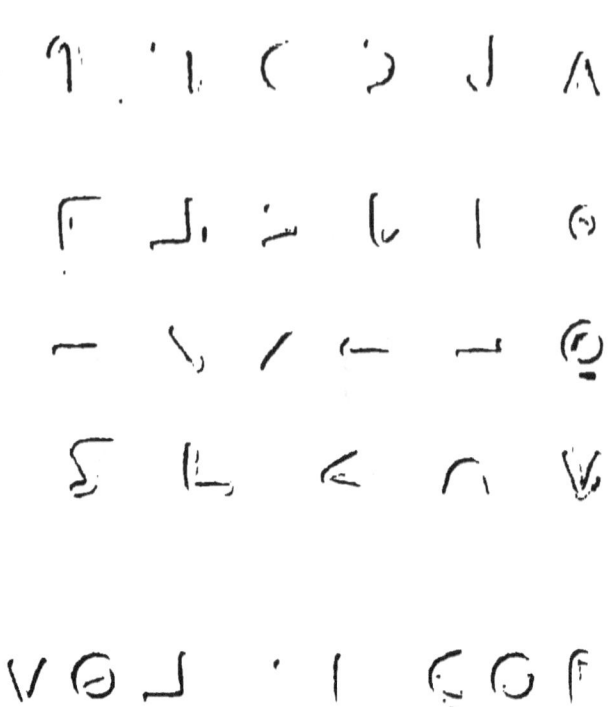

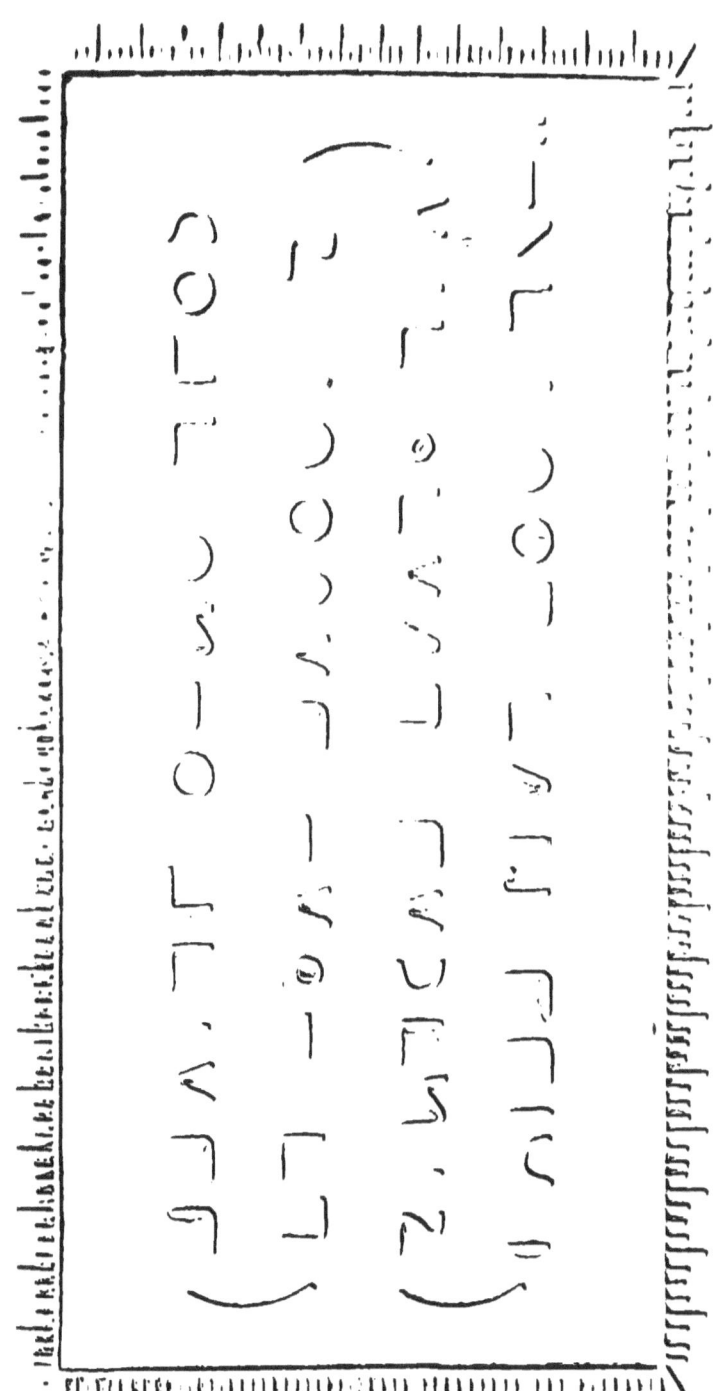

SPECIMEN OF READING IN MOON'S TYPE.

The first line is read from left to right and the second from right to left, to prevent the reader from losing his place.

MOON'S SOCIETY, 104, QUEEN'S ROAD, BRIGHTON.

Specimens of
Dr. Moon's Type for the Blind.

AS APPLIED TO FOREIGN LANGUAGES.

English,

OU\ ΓΛ—•Γ\ ∩•IC• Λ\— IN •ΓΛVΓN.

French,

N O —\Γ ⌐Γ\Γ →UI Γ/ ΛU> CIΓU>.

German,

U N/Γ\ VΛ—Γ\ IN ⊃Γꓶ •IꓶꓶΓL.

Dutch,

O N Z Γ VΛ⊃Γ\ .⊃IΓ IN ⊃Γ •ΓꓶΓLΓN

Danish,

VO\ VΛ⊃Γ\ .⊃U /Oꓶ I •IꓶLΓNΓ.

Swedish,

ΓΛ⊃Γ\ VΛ\ ./Oꓶ :Λ/— I •IꓶLOꓶ.

Russian,

O∩UL —Λ∩⌐ .C/∩ IΛ —Λ —LLLCΛ>⌐.

Arabic,

I—IUI IJΓ→ N→ IJΛΓOI/ J→/Zꓶ .Λ IΛΓS

Armenian,

∩⌐ <—JΓ V/Γ ∩Γ /ΓΛIN:>N /U.

Greek,

ΓN Λ\CΓ ΓN ⁚• L•ꓶ•/.

Hindustanee,

ΛI •Λꓶ˙Λ\Γ L˙Λ⌐: JO ˙Λ/ꓶ˙ΛN ⌐Λ\

Ningpo,

Λ• •LΛ• Λ••—IΛ LꙄ —ᶜIN ·Z⌐O∩ꓶ·ꓶO:

104, Queen's Road, Brighton.

Praise.

Words by Mrs. Moon.   *Music by* W. Moon, LL.D.

Lord Je - sus! let me talk with Thee Un - ceas - ing - ly the day;

For Thou art ev - er near to me With hosts of bright ar - ray!

CHORUS.

ff Glo - ry Hal - le - lu - jah! Glo - ry Hal - le - lu - jah!

Glo - ry Hal - le - lu - jah! Praise, Praise the Lord!

p Yes, Thou art every hope to me
Each name of sweetest rest :
And in Thy presence may I be
For *ever fully* blest !

When doubts and fears with lightning power
Strike on this trembling heart,
Thou say'st, "Although the tempests lower,
I ne'er from Thee will part."

And when heaven opens on the saint
Redeemed in Jesu's blood,
p No tongue can tell, no heart can paint
The glorious *rest* in *God !*

They "sleep in Jesus!"

"Them also which sleep in Jesus will God bring with Him."—1 THESS. iv. 14.

Words by MRS. MOON.

Music by W. MOON, LL.D.

p Sweet the slum-bers of the dead From the fount pe - ren - nial shed :

"Sleep in Je - sus!"—can there be Im - age so di - vine, that we

Sink in rap - ture in - to rest, Lean - ing on the Sa-viour's breast !

f Then the waking unto joy,
Ecstasies without alloy ;
Painless rapture, without tears
Wept along the course of years ;
Crystals of love, at every loss
Falling round the unchanged cross.

p Sweet the memory of those
Who ever in Christ repose,
Walk with Him arrayed in white,
Diademed with heavenly light,
Pouring their pent souls in praise,
Fountains streaming in Light's rays,

cres. Ever rising higher still,
Contemplating God's sweet will,
Satisfied that all was right
Viewed in the blaze of heaven's light :
ff Perhaps watching those they love
Waiting for their flight above !

THOUGHTS IN THE TRAIN FROM

BUXTON, JULY 22, 1887.

Jesus! I cling to Thee,
  For Thou hast died for me.
I trust my all to Thee,
  For Thou art *Love* to me.

Should death now come to me,
  Take me to Heaven with Thee
Thy glorious reign to see,
  Where life is stored for me.

If still I live for Thee,
  Let joy my portion be
By faith to rest in Thee,
  Till *sight* Thy face shall see!

A. M. M.

Letter received from W. HARRISON AINSWORTH, ESQ., *in acknowledgement of a copy of "A Family Memorial," containing additional information in reference to* DR. ELSDALE *and his Father.*

Little Rockley, Hurstpierpoint,

July 23, 1872.

My dear Mrs. Moon,

I have been absent from home, or I should have acknowledged, long before this, the very interesting "Family Memorial" which you have kindly sent me. Pray accept my best thanks for it! I am really very much pleased with the volume, which you have put together very charmingly, and in the best taste. The Literary Remains of your grandfather, the Rev. Wm. Leeves, well deserved to be collected. As the composer of the exquisite music of "Auld Robin Gray," he ought to have a niche in the Temple of Fame ; and I think these records will secure one for him. When he was an officer in the Foot Guards, in 1772, before he took Holy Orders, he must have been very handsome ; and his portrait, which is admirably engraved, adds to the attraction of the volume.

Naturally, I am very glad to possess a portrait of your father, Dr. Elsdale.

Mr. Robinson Elsdale, your Grandfather, appears to have been a very remarkable man. The volume (in MS.) containing his early adventures, was sent to me for publication by Dr. Elsdale. I lent it to Capt. Marryat, who based upon it his story, entitled " The Privateer's-Man." The early chapters of that Tale, are actually a transcript from your Grandfather's most curious narrative. Again thanking you for the interesting Memorial.   .

I remain, most sincerely yours,

W. HARRISON AINSWORTH.

In Memoriam.

THE REV. W. LEEVES,

AUTHOR OF THE AIR OF

"AULD ROBIN GRAY."

*OPINIONS OF THE PRESS: ON THE FIRST
EDITION.*

From the BRIGHTON OBSERVER, *December 5th,* 1873.

More than a century has passed away since the verses for
this old and ever to be popular air were written by Lady Anne
Lindsay, eldest daughter of the Earl of Balcarras. Amongst the
recent contributions to the beautiful Museum and Library with
which Brighton is now favoured, are two elegant volumes,—
published almost simultaneously,—one by Dr. Moon, the celebrated philanthropist of the Blind, and another by his consort,
Mrs. Moon, which is entitled, *In Memoriam, the Rev. W. Leeves,
Author of the air of " Auld Robin Gray."* One object in drawing
attention to the latter work is to point out to many of our
readers who may not be aware of it, the authorship of this
favourite air, especially as it is interesting to Brightonians to
know that Mrs. Moon is the grand-daughter of the composer.
In Memoriam contains (for the first time) a detailed history of
the ballad, accompanied by a reproduction of the original,

including the recitative, which is peculiarly interesting, it having been omitted in all the modern editions. The Rev. Wm. Leeves, in 1772, became a Lieutenant in the 1st Foot Guards, but afterwards took Holy Orders, and became Rector of Wrington, in 1779. In the musical world Mr. Leeves, says the *Bristol Mirror*, has immortalized himself by the exquisite and touching simplicity of the music of the pathetic ballad of "Auld Robin Gray," originally composed by him about 1770. It would appear, from the evidence Mrs. Moon has collected, that, although the names of the reputed authors were "legion," Mr. Leeves persisted for above 40 years in keeping his own claim to its origin from public notice ; and it was only when he was strongly persuaded by his friends,—especially Thomas Hammersley, Esq.,—that he publicly asserted his title to its authorship. Mrs. Moon's book is full of other matters of public interest. Amongst others, she refers to the labours of her uncle, the Rev. H. D. Leeves, B.D., Oxon, who was Chaplain to the Embassy at Athens, and who built the first Protestant church in that city. He also translated the Scriptures into modern Greek, 150,000 copies of which he was the means of circulating. It is additionally interesting to find from the companion volume,— *Light for the Blind*, by Dr. Moon,—that portions of these very Scriptures, in Greek, amongst eighty * other languages, have been rendered by him, in the embossed type, at his establishment in our own town. For many years the Rev. H. D. Leeves was engaged in the work of evangelization among the Greeks, by whom he was much beloved. A short memoir is also given of Mrs. Moon's father, the Rev. R. Elsdale, D.D.; who, after holding two Curacies and the Incumbency of Stretford, became High Master of the Manchester Free Grammar School. Although professedly only intended for "private circulation," this work is well worthy of more general perusal.

---

* Now 350.

THE COMPOSER OF "AULD ROBIN GRAY."

From the BRIGHTON TIMES, *December 6th,* 1873.

It will be interesting to Brightonians to know that the grand-daughter of the composer of the immortal air of "Auld Robin Gray," is Mrs. Moon, the wife of Dr. Moon, the talented blind philanthropist. A very handsomely got-up volume, by Mrs. Moon, entitled, *In Memoriam, the Rev. W. Leeves, Author of the air of " Auld Robin Gray,"* contains (for the first time) a detailed history of the ballad, accompanied by a reproduction of the original, including the recitative, which is peculiarly interesting, it having been omitted in all the modern editions. *In Memoriam* states that the Rev. Wm. Leeves, in 1772, became a Lieutenant in the 1st Foot Guards, but afterwards took Holy Orders, and became Rector of Wrington in 1779. Mrs. Moon also refers to the labours of her uncle, the Rev. H. D. Leeves, B.D., Oxon, who was Chaplain to the Embassy at Athens, and who built the first Protestant church in that city. He also translated the Scriptures into modern Greek, 150,000 copies of which he was the means of circulating. Portions of these Scriptures in Greek, amongst eighty* other languages, have been rendered by Dr. Moon, in his embossed type, at his establishment in our own town. For many years the Rev. H. D. Leeves was engaged in the work of evangelization among the Greeks, by whom he was much beloved. A short memoir of her father, the Rev. R. Elsdale, D.D., is also given; who, after holding two Curacies and the Incumbency of Stretford, became High Master of the Manchester Free Grammar School. Although intended only for "private circulation," this book is well worthy of more general perusal, by reason of the historical interest attached to the subject of the work, as well as by the care and ability displayed

---

* Now 350.

O

in this labour of filial love. We may add that a copy of this work, together with the companion volume, Dr. Moon's *Light for the Blind*, both very elegantly bound, have just been presented to the Brighton Museum and Library.

From the BRIGHTON EXAMINER, *January* 13*th*, 1874.

A FAMILY MEMORIAL. Dedicated to a Beloved Mother. Printed for private circulation.—Although it is hardly within the province of the critic to exercise his vocation with reference to works not published with the view of profit, but dedicated to domestic friendship, yet there are occasions, like the present, wherein nought but praise is due to the writer or compiler, where the rule may be legitimately dispensed with; and we are therefore pleased to give our voice in favour of this appropriate and valuable memorial. It is a very neatly got-up volume, which must be highly acceptable to the recipients, inasmuch as it contains family literary "remains," and notices of a beloved deceased grandfather of the compiler,—the Rev. W. Leeves,— poems by members of the family and friends, a brief sketch of the life of the Rev. Robinson Elsdale, D.D., &c., the whole being admirably illustrated by photographs of persons, places, and churches, familiar to the readers,—the members and friends of the family. A very interesting feature in the book is a solution of the question of the authorship of the beautiful old Scotch song, "Auld Robin Gray," one of the most exquisitely pathetic, both in music and words, of any similar composition extant. We quote some extracts with the view of giving what appears to have been the origin of the song. A quotation is given from a newspaper of the date of 1843, in which it is noticed, with respect to the song of

"AULD ROBIN GRAY,"

that "many persons who have sung or listened to this ballad, have thought all the while that they were singing or listening to genuine Scotch music, and an old Scotch ballad that had existed from the time they knew not when. No such thing. This air was originally and entirely composed by the Rev. William Leeves (who died only a few years ago), Rector of Wrington, in Somerset, and the friend and constant visitor of Mrs. Hannah More, at Barley Wood, in the same parish ; where the writer of this notice has often met both parties, and some of whose most pleasing reminiscences are associated with the old Rectory House, at Wrington, and its venerable and much-loved inmates. The son of this Mr. Leeves has long been settled at Athens, and some of our readers, have, we dare say, contributed to the church, which his and their means have conjoined to raise, and of which he is the zealous minister. It was the father of this Mr. Leeves, the Athenian, who, once an officer in the Guards, but afterwards, as we have said, the excellent rector of Wrington, having a great taste for music, on receiving the words of "Auld Robin Gray" at the hands of Lady Anne Lindsay, at her ladyship's special request (we believe there was a little wager pending relating to the possibility or not of closely imitating Scottish music) produced the beautiful ballad, which is now the theme of universal admiration, and as universally believed to be an original old air from the north of the Tweed ; for Mr. Leeves (giving himself up to the duties of his parish, and recreating himself with his violoncello and the composition of sacred music) gave no heed to the pirated editions which were springing up on all sides, and as little attention to the sensation it caused in the world."

From another newspaper the following is quoted :—

"In the life of Thomas Moore, by Lord John Russell, occurs the following passage :—

' Leaves, a clergyman, was the author of the words of ' Auld Robin Gray.' I already knew that Lady Anne Lindsay com- posed the music.'—*Lord John Russell's Life of Thomas Moore*, vol. 2, p. 180.

" Now the facts of the case are just the reverse. They are as follows, and we have good reason for knowing the truth of them.

Lady Anne Lindsay, looking over a volume of Ancient Scotch songs, admired an air, 'The bridegroom greets when the sun gangs down;' the words she did not much like, and wrote her touching ballad, 'Auld Robin Gray,' for adaptation to it. The Hon. Mrs. Byron, a friend of Lady Anne Lindsay, gave these lines to the late Rev. William Leeves (not Leaves), then a young officer of the Guards, afterwards (*cedant arma togæ*) Rector of Wrington, Somerset, who was uncle to the Rev. C. Eckersall. He (Mr. Leeves) did not know they had been arranged to this old Scotch air nor did he see it until quite late in life, after he had composed for them his beautiful recitative and air, so often and affectingly sung by the famed 'Kitty Stephens,' now Countess of Essex. The two airs have not the slightest resemblance to each other. There are numbers who still imagine the air to be an old Scotch one. Poor Wilson, who used to give such admirable illustrations of Scotch music, used to mention this fact in one of his delightful entertainments."

Another pleasing feature of the book is a copy of "Auld Robin Gray," as originally composed about the year 1770, by the Rev. William Leeves, with the words by the Lady Anne Lindsay. Both music and words will be interesting to the reader, as well from their intrinsic beauty as from other associations.

From the Brighton Guardian, *May 6th*, 1874.

In Memoriam, The Rev. W. Leeves, Author of the Air of "Auld Robin Gray," with a few notices of other members of his family. Printed for private circulation.

This family memorial consists of brief sketches of the lives, and of fragments in prose and verse, of the ancestors of the zealous and indefatigable editor, Mrs. A. M. Moon, wife of Dr. Moon, the celebrated philanthropist of the Blind, besides fugitive pieces in verse, and letters written by friends of the family. It is literally what its title implies, "A Family

Memorial," containing the authentication of the composer of the air to " Auld Robin Gray," which will be read with great interest. This fine song, so full of feeling, was written by Lady Anne Lindsay, about the year 1770. The Rev. W. Leeves, then a young officer in the 1st Foot Guards, received the words of the song from the Hon. Mrs. Byron, to whom they were presented by the authoress, and composed for them his beautiful recitative and air. From copies of the music given to friends, it found its way surreptitiously into print, and became very popular. Mr. Leeves left the army and became Rector of Wrington, in Somersetshire, the birth-place of Locke, and there became the friend of Hannah More, who resided in the neighbourhood. After a long period of 40 years, he claimed the melody, which had been considered Scotch, as his own. The book is well bound, and illustrated with photographs; that of Wrington Church, showing the house in which Locke was born, is very beautiful. There are letters written by Hannah More, and members of the Leeves family, also by Harrison Ainsworth to the editor, whose task in collecting and editing this " Family Memorial " is not only a proof of her piety and love, but of her literary zeal and ability.

www.ingramcontent.com/pod-product-compliance
Lightning Source LLC
Chambersburg PA
CBHW020115030726
47498CB00006B/2113